Love Whispered

The Love Series
Book #2

By:
Keta Kendric

Contents

Synopsis:

Callie: Trent stole my heart and shattered it into pieces when he disappeared without a trace. Time allowed me to puzzle the broken parts back together, but I was sure it would take an army to get me to surrender myself to another man... until Trent reappeared.

Trent: Callie deserved better than me. That's what I told myself when I walked out on the best thing to ever happen to me. All I had for a year were the whispers of what could have been...until the fates aligned and saw fit to give me another chance. However, the universe was determined to destroy the unraveling thread of hope that remained.

Warning: This is a multicultural contemporary romance that contains explicit language, explicit sexual content and is intended for adults.

Chapter One

Callie

The squeals of rolling laughter and the high-fiving between two female models drew my attention. I knew the reason for their excitement—knew that there was one person in this studio today who evoked that type of behavior and drew that much attention.

I would have to be the walking dead if I hadn't allowed my gaze to stray in *his* direction a time or two, maybe three. However, I was working, so gossiping about the hottest male model on set was never something I participated in.

The entertainment business boasted glitz and glamor, but it was one of the most vicious industries on the planet that chewed up models and spit them out daily. They allowed models like *him* fifteen minutes of fame, and if he were lucky, he would get a call back for another job.

"Ouch. Shoot," I hissed, sucking my pricked finger into my mouth after spearing it with the needle I'd worked through the seam of the shirt I was sewing. Keeping my finger in my mouth, I shoved my glasses up my nose with my middle finger while maintaining my place on the blouse I was preparing for the photoshoot already in progress.

One of the three models sandwiched between Twisted Minds, the band I currently designed clothes for, had been the topic of discussion on set all day. Several times, it appeared he'd glanced right at me and smiled.

I ignored him and maintained my worker bee status by keeping my head down and staying the hell out of people's way. It wasn't because I was shy either. If I was being honest, I didn't always like people and would rather not be bothered.

Nerdy, church mouse, and shy were some of the words tossed around to describe me. None of the names bothered me as long as I was allowed to do what I loved in peace.

The stampede of half-naked bodies heading my way yanked me back to reality. It was time for a clothing change. My designs were the main reason I was among this diverse group of singers, models, photographers, and other industry experts.

"Will you help me out of this, baby?" Minx, the lead singer of Twisted Minds, asked. Originally from New Orleans, she had a habit of calling everyone baby. The lazy sound of her accent put a smile on my face every time. Her smokey voice mixed with her southern twang was a uniquely appealing sound that shone through when she sang.

She lifted the top as far as it would go up her chest and arms, and I dragged it the rest of the way over her head. When the group first started out in the business, they sought out dressing rooms or private areas to change. Now, with time in the industry under their belt, modesty wasn't something they worried about as much.

"What do you want me in next?" Minx asked, trusting my judgment on her wardrobe choices down to her underwear. I reached back and picked up the shirt I had just added a few last-minute alterations to.

"This."

I lifted the tiny piece of blue material. The shimmery beading I added drew her gaze and put a smile on her face. While helping Minx into the top, I sensed eyes on me.

I instinctively glanced back, and my gaze landed on *him*. It wasn't the half-naked superstar in front of me he was looking at, either. The obscenely hot model I had convinced myself I imagined smiling at me earlier was looking directly at *me*.

Though reluctant to turn away from those hypnotically sexy, hazel-green eyes of his, I managed. His head of closely cropped, thick, dark brown hair and light eyes were a beacon that drew wanted and unwanted attention from every direction. His toned body was a full-length novel of sexually explicit fantasy that made ignoring him next to impossible.

Now that I was more aware of him, every move I made, whether pulling something from the racks to adjusting the clothing on the group's bodies, I could sense him assessing me.

Why?

Why was he looking at me? Did he like my clothing? Did he want me to design something for him? It wouldn't be the first time I'd been hired to create an exclusive private collection for someone who could afford it.

Hailee and Tangi, the other members of Twisted Minds, strolled up, their expectant eyes on me before landing on the rack stuffed with clothing next to me.

"Callie, I do believe you have an admirer," Tangi pointed out, smiling teasingly. I glanced up casually at the production team changing the scene for the next segment of the photo shoot that would take place on the stage.

"Who?" I finally asked, like the weight of his gaze wasn't still pressing down on me. I turned to Hailee, handing her a pair of shorts that would make her long legs stretch for miles.

"The *one*," Hailee hissed.

"I don't know his name, but he's all these lil' hot tail assistants, and female models keep rambling about. I happen to notice that he hasn't been paying them any mind because his eyes are on our little church mouse," Minx teased, poking me in the side.

"He probably sees what we see. The hot girl that's hiding under all those clothes and behind those glasses," Hailee continued, kicking off her heels.

"Are you going to talk to him? He does seem interested," Tangi asked, wiggling her way into the top I'd handed her.

"No. I'm here to make sure you ladies look fly as fuck. I don't have time to concentrate on him," I said, plucking a few pins from the sleeve of my top that I was using for a pin cushion.

"He probably just wants to see if he can get another notch on his endless bedpost anyway," I added under my breath.

What could have possibly been more interesting than the three sexy women I was dressing and undressing right in front of him? He was probably using the tactic of pretending to show interest in the most uninteresting person in the room to gain the attention of the one he truly wanted. If that were the case, his tactic was working because he was the flame, and they were the moths.

"Damn, Callie. You aren't even going to try? What if you're over here assuming, and he *sees* what others aren't patient or even smart enough to find?" Hailee asked, flashing me a stiff side-eye.

She was the hopeless romantic of the group who believed in love and soul mates despite all the riff-raff getting tossed her way where men were concerned.

"I'm good," I said, turning her for a better view of her top and bottoms together.

After the group was fully dressed, they strutted off together, checking out each other's outfits. I went on about the business of doing *my* business.

The unnerving sense of his assessing eyes followed me even as he stepped into the scene and awaited the camera snaps. One little telling thought climbed its way through all the denial I'd poured over it. I liked the attention. Liked that someone like him found interest in me.

I didn't suffer from self-esteem issues, but I worked in a world where beautiful people were a dime a dozen. Therefore, someone like me, who covered my body with my more conservative designs, often blended into the background. I preferred it that way since I saw firsthand what the constant spotlight could do to a person's life. I considered myself lucky enough to experience the limelight as an observer without actually suffering the harsh effects of its burn.

"Callie," Minx called, luring me back to reality. Damn, I hadn't even noticed that they had finished another segment of the shoot.

"Which one of these three dresses is mine?" she asked while Hailee and Tangie approached, already shedding shoes and accessories.

The next two hours went by in a blur of clothing changes, alterations, and the mix-and-match game of all the clothing I had created for this amazing group. This photoshoot was one of the biggest they had landed. Hailee and Tangie were originally from Richmond, Virginia, like me. They, along with Minx, shared a home right outside the city for the past few years.

When they told me they had landed a six-page spread in Legacy Magazine a month ago, my heart burst with pride. That wasn't the kicker though. They had turned down the better-known designer the magazine suggested to allow me to dress them for the shoot.

The incredible gesture made me ugly cry. I balled my damn eyes out like a baby for hours after receiving the news. With this shoot and the group's fast-climbing popularity, my designs were attracting major attention.

The group was so taken aback by my ideas and the clothing I made that they presented me with a contract to work with them exclusively for two years. I was floored by their offer to keep me employed for anything beyond a year. They'd even asked for three years, but at some point, I wanted to drive my career down a few other avenues. For what they were paying me, plus my end-of-year bonuses, I almost signed the longer contract.

My career was the ultimate labor of love, starting with me dressing my dolls and cutting up my clothing to make outfits for my plastic children.

For years, I'd managed to fight through all of the teasing from schoolmates and negative criticism from people in general. I didn't fit the societal beauty standard, nor did I fit into the fashion industry's standard, so I, as well as my designs were ignored.

I wasn't thin enough, my skin wasn't light enough, and my face was too plain to be in an industry that thrived on beauty. I was told that design was a hobby, something I'd grow out of, that it wasn't a career.

I, on the other hand, didn't care what they said. Something within me wouldn't accept their unsolicited advice or negative opinions. The passion that flowed through me like the blood in my veins was what I fought to make them see, my designs, my clothing.

The hard work and dedication was finally paying off, and the two people who supported me from day one, my best friends Charlene McGregor and Dayton Davis, remained at my side for every step I took to reach my dreams.

Chapter Two

Callie

"I believe you are the hardest working person in this building," came a male voice.

I jumped, despite him standing right in front of me. He was so close that the sudden sound of his voice scared the heck out of me.

With my hand covering my chest, my breaths blowing out fast and hard, I hit *him* with a wide-eyed *what-the-hell* expression.

"I'm sorry I scared you. You appeared to be looking right at me, but I suppose you were deep in thought?" he surmised.

I nodded. "Yes. Sometimes, I'm consumed with design ideas, and I give into the images and allow myself time to process what I see."

He was here, talking to me, and *wow*, he was even better looking up close than he was from afar. That smile of his was genuine and deepened the longer I stared at him.

"I don't know much about design, but your clothes are like pieces of art. Each is precise with its own spark of personality. Kind of like people with their own individual identity."

My lips parted at his unexpected and elegantly expressed compliment. If he was trying to win me over, it was starting to work.

"Thank you. I appreciate you noticing my work."

He reached out his hand.

"Trenton Pierce, but please call me Trent."

A first, last, and preferred name. What did *that* mean?

I took the hand he offered and noticed how his large hand closed firmly around my small one. My reddish-brown was swallowed up by his light beige. His hand was warm, soft, and strong, and his touch was indescribably *familiar*.

He didn't let go of my hand right away, allowing me to concentrate on our connection. The sizzle radiating into my palm spread like warm honey all over me. There was a palpable energy flowing off of him that continued to thread its way through our connection and made me hang on to his hand a lot longer than I intended. I needed to say something before he decided I was a weirdo.

"Callie," I finally replied, lifting my gaze before I made things awkward by the way I was staring at our hands. His up-close presence sparked my curiosity despite my earlier impression of him. The man looked too good to be true and I noticed a few details of what made me think so in the first place.

"Not my business, but you shave...everything?" It was more a statement than a question and telling of how much I'd checked him out during the day. Male models were known to shave certain parts for photo shoots, but it appeared Trenton shaved everything all over.

"Yes. When I'm not volunteering myself as someone's part-time prop in photos, I'm also a dancer, which is a different type of prop altogether."

There was a slice of regret in his gaze and a dip in his tone when he said he was a dancer, letting me know he wasn't a Broadway professional. I believe he expected me to express disappointment when he volunteered what he did for a living. When I didn't comment, he continued.

"Dancing under all that light shows everything, so making my skin as clean as possible puts a glow on it that makes it appear perfect.

"It does look perfect. I believe you would...I mean, it would look great under any light," I blurted, not thinking about how my comment may sound before I blabbed it.

His smile, straight and pearly white, brightened the room.

"Thank you."

He stared hard like he was studying me or decoding something I wasn't aware I was putting out.

"So, what are you doing when you get off this evening?" he asked, his dazzling eyes sparkling and as persuasive as his smile.

"I'm dragging myself into the shower first. Then, I'm going to do a swan dive into my bed. Sleep is calling, and I'm answering it."

He chuckled. "You deserve it. It wasn't a line when I said you are the hardest working woman in this building."

A moment of odd silence fell between us, and only our eyes moved in mutual...*something*. Was it admiration I saw in his gaze?

The edgy feeling he'd set loose on me lingered, making me wring my hands to ease the tingling currents. Was he experiencing the same? He kept drumming his fingers against his leg.

"How do you like the quick pace of New York compared to the easy stroll of Virginia?"

My forehead creased, and the strange impulse to step back took control. He held up his hands at my reaction.

"I am not a stalker. I just know that you're from Richmond, and so am I. A few of the other models here today also are. When Twisted Minds was home a month ago, they saw some of us dance at Club Quiet Chaos. Their manager made us an on-the-spot deal for a modeling gig. For a while, I didn't think it was legit because it was so out of the blue, but proper paperwork was delivered, and contracts were offered."

"Congratulations. Is modeling something you've always wanted to do?"

He shook his head. "No, I consider myself lucky. At twenty-seven, I'm well past the age of modeling. However, in the past few years, I've been on five shoots, and, along with dancing, it pays my bills and tuition."

The bit of news about tuition made my smile widen. It was a hint that he wanted more than to dance and model.

"What are you going to school for?" My curiosity had gotten the better of me. I was supposed to be gearing up to leave and enjoy my free weekend of rest and relaxation in the luxurious Manhattan hotel paid for by my wonderful employers. Yet, Trent held my interest hostage.

"Information Technology. I started college when I was nineteen. I went a solid two years but had some problems that wiped me out financially. School had to take a back seat until I got myself together."

He paused for a long time. I could tell he was contemplating telling me something heavy based on the way his head tipped down and his shoulders dropped. There was also a flash of embarrassment peeking from the depths of his pretty eyes.

"I was addicted to drugs. It took me two tries at recovery to kick and start facing life's problems head-on versus dulling my senses with drugs."

He probably expected me to judge him for giving in to the temptation of drugs, but I didn't. Everyone had their demons, but some people's demons happened to be bigger and more horrifying than others. I usually observed more than I spoke, listened more than I gave my opinion, and, therefore, picked up more details when people talked to me. Casting judgment, especially on someone I didn't know, wasn't wise.

"I'm glad you were able to get help and allow yourself to heal," I finally told him.

His smile returned, shining brighter this time. A spark of genuine gratitude for my words rested in his gaze. I suspected he was used to getting judged or receiving negative feedback for being honest about something I knew was hard for him to confess.

"Three years ago, I returned to school. I applied and was accepted into grad school this year."

My brows lifted. He wasn't just a pretty face and hot body, he was slaying his demons and chasing his dream.

"That's an amazing accomplishment, Trent. Congratulations again."

I hesitated, not sure how to question him about dancing, although curiosity was burning a hole in my tongue.

"Dancing helps you…financially? Does it pay well?" I spit out the questions. I'd only been to a handful of strip clubs, and although it appeared the men made a lot of money, rumors were that the house took most of it.

"Yes. Without dancing, I wouldn't have been able to go to college at all. I wouldn't have been able to help my mother financially. It's not the career path I wanted to take, but it came along at a time when I didn't have anything else. In a way, it saved me."

The more I talked to Trent, the more personable he became. He wasn't a prop or the stereotype that some, me included, lumped dancers into. Although I wasn't fully convinced that his motivations were genuine where I was concerned, his conversation intrigued me enough to keep talking.

Chapter Three

Trent

The broad smile on my lips hadn't left my face since we left the studio. Usually, I would already be at some hotel, buried deep inside a woman whose name I would have already forgotten. But not with Callie. She was interesting in a way that snatched my attention when I was convinced that women were all the same.

"I'm glad you decided to have coffee with me. For a minute, I thought I'd have to get down on my knees and beg."

She chuckled flatly.

"I mean, no offense, but men who look like you aren't knocking down my door. And I'm woman enough to know what it means that you are."

I lifted a brow at her straightforward statement.

"What? What does it mean?" I asked, genuinely wanting to know what she believed my interest in her meant. I was also curious to understand her perception of the way she thought I saw her.

"One, you're interested in a one-and-done kind of night. Two, you're curious about what I might be like in bed since I'm probably not the usual type of woman you date. Three, there is something you want me to do for you like designing some free clothes or something. I don't know which it is, but I'm not naive enough to think otherwise."

My eyes, pinned on hers, widened at her candor.

"You are direct. I like it. But…"

She lifted a hand. "Please, spare me the lines and lies. We are going to make this," she waved a hand between me and her. "...A lie-free zone."

"You're not wrong. Given my line of work and what I prefer, I've only ever been interested in brief hook-ups. One night has worked well in avoiding the drama that always seem to get dragged into relationships. I'd rather not deal with any of it," I told her honestly.

She hadn't turned her nose up, gotten up, and walked away yet. Instead, she nodded, digesting my brutally honest confession.

I also found her overwhelmingly interesting, and though she was dressed conservatively and wore glasses, it didn't make her any less beautiful. If anything, it made me appreciate that she didn't have to use skimpy clothing and a face full of makeup to catch my attention.

However, telling her so after her statement would only make me look like a big fat liar. It would also imply that because I find her so interesting and beautiful, my customary one-night stand didn't apply to her. Although she possessed a quiet confidence about herself and an unusually perceptive idea about my temporary desires, I didn't want there to be any misunderstandings about my short-term dating preference.

"I can respect that," she finally said after chewing on the statement I'd voiced. "If living your relationships through one-night increments is what fits your life, I'm not here to judge you. I'm also not looking for anything steady. My career is starting to take off and doesn't leave much time to invest in a relationship. Besides, I just got out of a situation-ship three months ago, and my ex-boyfriend's behavior encouraged me to stay single for as long as necessary."

I smiled.

"Are you okay with us being just one night?" I asked while my voice of reason screamed, *"Are you crazy? She's worth more than one night."*

"One night," she repeated.

"One night," I reiterated, smiling like we had just made an unbreakable pact.

***

She kept staring around the little diner I had chosen, her big pretty brown eyes casting an endless depth that I became lost in several times. Callie was different, innocent almost. No matter how many times I convinced myself that she was just another woman, the lie would not stick.

"I didn't expect this," she said, finally facing me across the little cozy booth. It was late, after ten-thirty, and the only place I could think to bring her that you didn't need a reservation for was a little diner called Queen's that I'd eaten at the last time I was in the city.

"I like it," she said, allowing a smile to creep across her face. I figured she would. I'd been eye-stalking her closely all day. She appreciated more retro styles and incorporated a lot of creations from the past into the clothing she designed. The diner was a replica from the fifties, down to the little jukebox on our table.

She flipped through the music before digging inside her little handbag for some coins. A quarter got her three songs, but her fingers slid too quickly across the little keys to see what she'd chosen.

The waitress, a brunette woman in her thirties, walked up in her pinstriped uniform. The bottom portion of the uniform flared out like the poodle skirts from that era and stopped right below her knees. She even had on white bobby socks and black and white saddle shoes.

She stood at the head of our table, popping her gum and dancing to Johnny Cash's 'Folsom Prison Blues' that began to play from some hidden speakers inside the place.

"Hello. Here are your menus." She slapped two laminated sheets on the table. "Just wave me over when you're ready to order."

Since there were only two other occupied tables, getting the waitress's attention wouldn't be hard. Before she stepped away, I handed her a five.

"Can we get more coins for the jukebox? My girlfriend is enjoying the music." The woman's smile widened at my words, but she managed to keep her gum popping with every other breath she took. She shoved the five into the pockets of her apron. "Sure thing, hun," she replied before marching away. The waitress may have been all smiles, but the only one that mattered to me at this moment was Callie's.

Another couple entered, making the little bell above the door chime. It was two men, lovers based on the way they were glued to each other's side. They flashed smiles and gave a little wave in our direction that we returned before they took the table three down from ours.

The waitress placed the coins on our table as she walked past us to help the couple.

"They say you should never assume, but I thought you would be all about getting back to my or your place so we can get this night over and done with," Callie blurted.

"See, that's what you get for assuming things." I pointed a finger at her. "I actually enjoy your company. I like talking to you. And despite what we agreed to, you don't look at me like I'm just meat or an object."

Her brows knitted like my statement disturbed her.

"Is that how women make you feel? Like you're just…meat?"

I nodded.

"Yes. More than you can possibly imagine. I know it has a lot to do with my jobs, and I understand that I'm being paid to be treated a certain way. But, when I leave the walls of the club or a studio, I'm still a person who wants to be taken seriously. I want my ideas to be heard and taken into consideration. However, I still manage to only be seen as a thing," I told her.

I shrugged. I wasn't the most articulate person, but I prayed Callie didn't take my words as whining and at least understood what I was trying to say.

"You said I don't look at you like you're just meat. How do I look at you? Isn't agreeing to this one-night hook-up putting myself in the category with everyone else?"

I shook my head slowly. "No. You have no idea everything that I've pick up from you. Your expressions hold a genuine interest in them when you talk to me. You *listen* to what I have to say and respond with genuine replies, ideas, and emotion. Your words are kind, not innuendo or lines meant to lead to the quickest way to get me into bed. You use your eyes to engage with me and not to undress me."

The level of intrigue and the smile flashing in her gaze said she fully understood my words and enjoyed them, so I continued.

"Tonight, I convinced you to be with me when it's usually the other way around. I attract a lot of attention, and some I entertained because, if I'm being honest, it's good for the type of business I'm in. However, most of the attention I receive I don't crave because it doesn't mean anything. Despite my confidence in myself, it still stings when I'm treated like an alien species whose only purpose is to satisfy sexual desires. Most don't even see me as someone with the capacity to learn and elevate myself beyond sex, muscles, and a nice body."

Callie sat slack-jawed, her eyes searching mine, and I'm sure finding the seriousness in what I'd just revealed. She reached across the table and sat her hands atop mine. The care in her eyes reached into me and stroked a cord of emotions I didn't know I possessed. 'Earth Angel' by The Penguins played softly in the background, a meaningful tribute to the beautiful woman sitting in front of me.

"We can just talk and enjoy each other's company. We don't have to do this one-night hook-up. I don't want to treat you like the rest of them because I don't see you as just an object that's supposed to deliver sex. I don't want you walking away from me, feeling like you're not even human. That's too...heavy. It's heartbreaking."

My throat tightened at the sight of tears starting to form in her eyes. She'd felt the essence of my message deep enough to reveal to me the emotions they elicited.

"You're sitting in front of me, listening to me, empathizing with a part of my reality that I hate. It is a part that I deal with by swallowing the rawness of it and pulling from the few good parts. There was no way I was leaving that studio without you tonight. Your spirit. Your whole vibe. It was why I was the one who made the move this time. I want to be with you. I like you. You're nothing like them, never will be."

I turned my hands to hold hers before closing them into mine.

"Callie, I have been with a lot of women. My body count is...extensive." The too-honest statement concerned her, and though she fought to keep the emotion from spilling into her eyes, it peaked.

"I'm not telling you this to scare you. You can be assured I'm always safe, and I take care of my health."

She nodded.

"I told you that because of how often I'm hit on, picked up on, treated like a sexual vending machine, and I'm talking about outside the club. No costume, no bare chest, no sexual performances. I often say yes to these dates, half the time because I'm bored, but if I'm being honest with myself, I do it as a small form of rebellion against the total lack of disregard that some women have for me."

She squeezed my hands. The Platters', 'Only You' was playing now.

"I assumed you enjoyed the attention. But I understand now that the situation goes much deeper than that for you. I will admit, I'm still struggling to understand some of it—to wrap my head around it all," she said.

She fixed her gaze straight ahead, staring at nothing, thinking. I believe she was trying to reconcile how I said I felt with what made sense to her.

"The attention you receive has no emotional or meaningful intentions attached to it, so it's like white noise to you. Here's a scenario. It's like the difference between a woman coming up to you and telling you you're the hottest man in the world and walking away without wanting or needing anything in return from you for the compliment, and one blatantly undressing you with her eyes and tossing you her hotel room keycard, expecting her sexual fantasy to get fulfilled. You have only ever gotten the latter, though you would prefer the first."

I nodded. "You truly do see me. You have no idea how it feels to be seen as more than just..."

"...Meat." she finished. She pointed a finger into her chest.

"I'm on the other end of the spectrum. I'm only a hot commodity for certain men who prefer a more subdued type of woman. I think I give off a strong, nerd-like vibe. And although I don't get as much attention as some, I'm okay with that because it means that the ones I do get attention from actually *see* me."

I leaned across the table, letting her hand go and calling her closer with a wave of my finger. We met in the middle, our faces inches apart.

"You are a hell of a lot more than a nerdy vibe, Callie. You are a beautiful woman, and I'm seriously attracted to you."

"Seriously?" she asked, her brows lifting, a smile shining in her eyes.

"Yes. Can I kiss you now?"

She didn't answer, but the sensual slide of her tongue across her bottom lip, her nostrils flaring, and the gleam of uncut lust in her eyes was all the answer I needed. Being this close, her energy had a hold of me.

Our lips met, soft flesh moving gently until the connection sparked and ignited something intensely exhilarating that I'd never experienced. The beautiful tension fluttered low in my belly and lifted closer to my chest with each languid motion of her lips against mine.

I wanted to enjoy the luxurious sensation of her body against mine. I needed more. We, me, or just her, deepened the kiss. I couldn't tell. The hard press urged me to send my tongue across her lips before it slipped into her mouth.

Shit.

The sweet, hot flow of this kiss, the emotional high, the tingly sensations rolling through my body and dancing along my skin. I eased back, dazed and breathing erratically with wide eyes. Her dazed expression indicated that she was as shaken up as my rattling insides indicated that I was. Her eyes hung heavy in her head from the…the…

What the hell was this?

Someone's throat cleared, and my neck snapped up to the waitress standing at our table. Her lips were drawn into a tight ball from her fighting not to laugh at our total disregard for our surroundings.

"Are you two ready to order, and if so, should I make it to go?"

I glanced at Callie. She nodded, and I wasn't sure which of the waitress's questions she was saying yes to.

Callie cleared her throat, her eyes lingering on me before she allowed them to drop to the forgotten menu.

"Double cheeseburger with everything, half fries, half onion rings with a lemonade," she said, looking up at the waitress with that inviting smile of hers.

"Oh, and will you add the apple pie," she decided, tapping the menu.

"Everything she just said," I told the gum-popping waitress when she glanced in my direction for my order.

"Coming right up," she said before turning to walk off.

"Will you make that all to-go?" Callie called after the woman, who glanced across her shoulder and winked.

"Thought so," she said, marching toward the section of the counter that opened to the kitchen to put in our order. The Flamingos', 'I Only Have Eyes For You' spilled into the space, a fitting song since I couldn't keep my eyes off the beautiful woman sitting across from me.

We sat through Ray Charles', ' I Got A Woman', Frank Sinatra's, 'I've Got You Under My Skin', and The Platters', 'Only You' before the waitress came bouncing back in our direction with our order.

I couldn't let go of the sensational high that the kiss sparked. I wanted more, a lot more than her kisses. Now, I fought tooth and nail to keep flashes of our naked bodies from the depths of my damn triggered brain cells.

After I paid the waitress, Shirley & Lee's, 'Let The Good Times Roll' was our exit theme music.

Chapter Four

Callie

The twinkle of the city lights gave way to the smooth melody of honking horns, rumbling voices, and the faint sound of a distant subway car squeaking along the tracks. The noise made sense in this city, sounding more like a natural song than the ever-churning living chaos it breathed.

"I never thought I'd be sitting on the balcony overlooking Manhattan on a Friday night having dinner with a gorgeous guy. This is pretty amazing," I blurted out, saying what was supposed to stay in my head. However, I had nothing to lose by speaking truthfully to Trent. We would never see each other again after tonight.

He lifted his glass of wine he'd poured from the complimentary bottle from the hotel. "Here's to us and to making the most of the time we have with no regrets."

Our glasses clinked.

"No regrets," I repeated the toast.

And with him, I sensed that he would make sure I had a good, no regrets, kind of night. We sipped our wine and ate our calorie-laced burgers and fries with gusto, licking our lips and ketchup-laced fingers.

The food was good, and the conversations we had about nothing and everything were on point. There was no denying the underlying chemistry stirring between us.

I had to admit that I was not used to a man this damn fine giving me this much attention. The sense that he wasn't doing it *just* to get into my panties made this encounter one-of-a-kind.

This feels too real, the little voice deep in the back of my mind whispered.

I shook off the idea, breaking the swirling symphony in my head, repeating that our chemistry was real. I stood and walked to the balcony before panning down from the view of skyscrapers to observe the scene below.

This place truly never slept. The buzzing flow of traffic and people were a living example of infinity.

Warm hands slid around my waist before a strong, tall body I'd been feasting my eyes on all day pressed against the back of mine. The stiff press of his dick into my lower back had me fighting back a grin. We both knew it was time to do something about the heavy tension that had been swirling between us all day.

The gentle press of his lips to the side of my neck drew a low moan from me while his arms encircled me fully from behind. He spun me to face him, our eyes meeting, searching and telling stories we didn't say out loud. The smile in his gaze grew into a glint of lust he didn't hide.

His desire for me became a physical presence, flowing off him in an invisible breeze that raised goosebumps on my arms. All it took was for him to lean in, and our lips meshed into a sweet tango of soft presses and languid sucks that enticed a chorus of soft moans.

The lower part of my body rocked from side to side, my legs working against each other to relieve the heavy tension growing in my sex. Trent reached for my glasses.

"Can you see without these?"

I nodded, biting my lip while watching him take my glass and sit them some place behind us. Trent lifted me high so that my legs wrapped around his waist, but it was where he'd placed my ass that drew a loud gasp from me.

"Trent," I called, glancing back and over the balcony.

"I'm not going to let you fall," he whispered before his lips claimed mine again and stole my attention away from what was behind me.

Nothing.

His strong hands and my legs around his waist were my safety nets. There was a brick privacy wall between us and the neighbors on either side of us. However, if those people decided to step onto their balcony to enjoy the view, they might see and hear more than they bargained for.

Why did the idea of them hearing or even seeing us turn me on? Never having been in this situation before, I found this act highly enticing, and it helped spike my desires.

Trent's kisses made me forget about the ledge my ass sat perched atop. Thankfully, I wasn't scared of heights, or this sexy encounter would have been going differently. He lowered my legs, and our height difference, me at five-seven and him at least six-two, had me glancing up as he assisted me in sliding off the ledge until I stood on shaky legs in front of him.

We didn't ask permission, he tugged at my clothes, and I yanked his apart. We were a tangle of arms and material being stretched and flung in every direction. Tops off, I licked my lips at the sight of me unbuttoning his jeans and slipping his zipper down.

After toeing off his shoes, he placed his hand atop mine and helped me not only take his jeans down but his boxers as well. My eyes bucked at the thick peachy flesh of his dick starting to peak.

"Stop," he commanded, and I froze. Had I done something wrong?

He reached down and tugged his wallet from his back pocket, removing a condom and flashing me a quick wink. He placed his hands back atop mine so we could continue the job of getting his pants and boxers off.

With his assistance, the clothes went down his body fast enough that I bent to keep from going down to the floor with the pants. My face stopped inches from where he popped out.

"Holy hell."

Had I said that out loud? I had no idea, but it was all that came to mind to describe him. The man packed a serious portion of prime-cut meat. It was enough to make me squirm harder but for a different reason this time. I swallowed, my eyes glued to him—stiff and proudly aimed right at my mouth.

"Callie," he called, getting my attention. "Aren't you going to finish getting me out of these jeans?"

"Oh," I said, shaking off the hypnotizing effect before ripping my eyes away from his thick, long, and very intimidating dick. "Yeah," flew out of my mouth while I worked the pants the rest of the way off his legs and over his feet. When I finished my task, my eyes resumed their job of staring at his dick. I couldn't help myself.

He had no trouble getting me out of my pants, taking my drenched panties down with them. I held on to his shoulders and enjoyed how his eyes danced appreciatively over my body. I wouldn't describe myself as slender, but I wasn't thick either. My ass filled out a pair of sized ten, and my C-cups gave me enough in the front to entice male eyes.

He didn't get back up after taking my pants off and tossing them aside. Without warning, he slipped a hand under my right thigh and lifted my leg so damn fast my hands flew back and caught the thick bricks of the balcony my ass had just been planted on. He slung my leg across his shoulder and glanced up.

What a view.

A man so hot he could melt my panties clean off my body was between my legs, glancing up at me with a smirk that said he was about to eat me like his favorite meal. I never wanted to wake up from this fantasy. This view would forever be embedded in my head. This gorgeous man, kneeling before me, with one of my legs dangling across his shoulder and his mouth inches from my mound.

"My bad," he said with a sly grin. "I almost forgot to ask permission."

All I could do at this point was swallow because this couldn't have been happening to me.

"Can I eat your pussy?"

I nodded, my head jerking up and down so fast that it surprised me that my vertebrate didn't click.

"Oh," poured past my lips like warm honey at the first sensational lick. It was the only discernible word I could get out because Trent went to town on my pussy, not leaving a spot, a space, or a piece untouched.

He lifted my other leg, keeping it penned open to allow him to control the full bottom half of my body while my elbows dug into the flat brick surface of the balcony. When the first finger slipped inside me, my eyes crossed in my head, but when that second finger slid in and stretched me wider, my damn uterus cried, and my walls quivered right along with my inner thighs.

Trent drove me into my orgasm so smoothly that I didn't know if I was crying or shouting.

He stood, repositioning my shaking legs so they ended up around his waist. The hard press of his dick against my sensitive nub and the wanton area he'd prepared so well gave me a sense of bravery I didn't know I possessed.

He moved us, turning us to the brick wall that separated us from the neighbors. We were in danger of being seen and heard, more now than on the balcony, because of the brick-sized cut-outs in the wall.

I slipped my hand inside one of the spaces to have something to hold on to while the top of my back pressed into the surprisingly smooth, hard surface. At a glance, I noticed the condom was already in place. Why did his dick look even bigger than before?

He aligned us and kept his eyes on mine, my legs spread wide from the way he palmed my inner thigh with one of his hands while his opposite hip pushed my other leg open.

Right when the head licked across my clit and lowered to my dripping wet folds, my eyes slammed shut.

"Wait. Why are you doing that?" he questioned, concern edging out in his tone.

I peeled my eyes open.

"Doing what?" I asked, my breathing labored, my chest heaving in anticipation.

"You look like you're afraid it's going to hurt."

My cheesy grin spread wider.

"You're bigger than I'm used to, and despite you making me dripping wet...you're *big*."

"I can promise that I'll not hurt you. I don't care if it takes an hour. I'll work it in so slowly that you'll be begging me for more in no time."

My top teeth bit deep into my bottom lip, and my gaze dropped to his dick before I lifted it to meet his again. He'd misunderstood me.

I peered at him through my heavy gaze and whispered, "I *want* it to hurt."

His lips parted on a silent *'O'* before a wicked grin appeared. His sudden thrust, fast, hard, and deep, knocked the breath clean from my lungs.

The shock. The pain. The delicious pleasure.

"Fuck!" he shouted, glancing down at where our bodies were connected. My muscles clenched so hard that the ache shot through me like lightning. When he backed out and repeated the deep hard stroking, I lost my natural damn mind.

Legs shaking, ass twerking, hips flexing, tits bouncing, eyes wide open one minute and slamming shut the next, nails scraping the skin off his shoulder and probably pieces of brick from the spot I gripped.

When he stopped his aggressive pounding, my eyes flew open, and all that screaming and moaning I was doing turned into a vicious side-eye.

"It's your turn. I want you to ride me in this position."

How the hell am I going to do that?

While still deep inside me, Trent inched me higher up his body so that my legs locked around his waist. He pried my hands from his shoulder and my nails out of his skin before lifting my stiff hands above my head to another opening. I hung on once my fingers connected and my hands found something I could grip.

He reached around my waist and gripped my ass. Lifting, he gave me another boost that allowed my legs to loosen and widen so he could slide deeper. Now, I got it. I moved the lower half of my body against his. It felt unnatural at first, but I found a rhythm that allowed me to use his dick in the best possible way. He stretched and massaged everything I wanted and needed.

Making me ride him like this was something I'd never done before, but he somehow knew that I would like it. I would be sore tomorrow because I used every damn muscle I had, ass, abs, hips, and even chest to make the thick piece of pulsing heat inside me kiss every slippery inch of my walls all the way down until his head licked the very core of me.

"So...deep," I breathed out on a long-winded exhale. And in my ravenous state, I wanted him deeper. I don't know what vibes our connection gave off, but he must have sensed my carnal desire because he tightened his hold on my hips and managed to push them higher, aiming my knees at the wall.

He backed halfway out, and the sight of him hard, veiny, and slick with my juices sent a devilish thrill through me before he pushed himself back inside. The hard impact of the thrust shocked me at first until a river of fiery hot sensation took my ability to think straight.

He repeated the process of backing out to gain momentum and pounding into me with a force that allowed him in so deep it knocked loud gasps from my throat each time. My spine tingled, and my lady parts were a symphony of vibrations so strong they hummed through the rest of my body.

"That's it, baby, take it all."

He caught my bottom lip between his teeth and dragged them along the tender flesh of my lip as his dick dragged unapologetically along my walls. Whatever tension my body was attempting to hold on to had vacated the premises, and he maintained full control of me.

The best I could do was to keep my arms slung loosely across his shoulders, unable to recall when my hands had come off the wall.

Trent fucked me. Deep. Hard. And with a purpose that had me screaming, "Oh God. Trent," on repeat.

I didn't climax. I didn't come. My ass ascended into a whole new light—one that overdosed me on the gloriously astonishing fusion of pure pleasure and explicit bliss.

"Damn, Callie. Fuck!" Trent shouted, but my rolling moans continued, drowning out his pleasure-filled cries.

When reality began to settle with him pressed tightly against my shivering body, I peeled one eye open, finding him looking at me with a glint of astonishment in his heavy gaze. Our breaths, still getting the better of us, mingled, along with the buzz of our sex hanging heavy in the air.

"Oh my God. What..." My ability to think straight hadn't come fully back online. "How...what did you do to me? I've never..."

"...Come that fucking hard," he finished. "Me either. That was...um..."

Apparently, I wasn't the only one attempting to figure out how to string a sentence together.

"That was a whole new level," he managed to say, staring wide-eyed like I was the one who had made our sex that explosive.

The saga continued inside the hotel room, the shower, the little kitchenette, and finally ended with us in bed, exhausted enough to fall into a deep, peaceful sleep.

Chapter Five

Callie

The next day, Saturday, we enjoyed breakfast in bed thanks to the hotel's excellent breakfast choices. We spent some time enjoying more conversations, from bold and funny to intense and meaningful.

Neither of us mentioned that our one-night stand was spilling into the next day. To say something would mean that it would have to end, so we were choosing to ignore the elephant in the room.

Later, we abandoned the hotel room and went out to lunch after stopping briefly at my hotel room for a change of clothes. I even convinced Trent to hop on one of those double-decker bus tours because I wanted a wider view of the New York area. The two-hour adventure turned out to be an education in culture as much as the sights captured my interest.

By the time evening rolled around, we'd decided to dine at the fancy restaurant inside the hotel, enjoying a phenomenal meal of creamy spinach-stuffed salmon with coconut rice that I would remember and seek out whenever I visited the city again.

We styled each other's hair, binged TV shows, and bathed in the big garden tub together, which led to a hot and splashy sex scene. We massaged each other, mainly him rubbing my sore muscles and me wanting to get my hands on his tantalizing body.

The sex we managed to fit into the day was as out of this world as it had been the night before.

I caved in to all the good vibes swirling between us and thought less and less about the short timeline we'd agreed to but were not mentioning out loud.

***

Sunday came along and brought with it a lingering sadness at the notion that our time was dwindling. We were scheduled to fly home tomorrow, so today was all we had. We still hadn't mentioned how our one night had turned into a weekend. The unspoken spoke louder and reached further than any words we could ever say.

Reality reared its ugly head, and I allowed the looming notion of never seeing Trent again to get the best of me.

There was something about him that resonated with me. I didn't have to force myself to have fun. It just happened. Our conversations were natural and could flow on forever if we didn't stop ourselves. He didn't look at me like our time was all about sex. His intentions with me, though put on a strict timeline, felt lasting and meaningful.

I was usually tense during sex—anxious in a way that didn't always make it enjoyable. My unease would often compel the guy to get his and go, and I was left wanting something more, something different. Not with Trent. I responded to him in a way I'd never experienced. He made me want the sex and crave it so desperately I would forget all inhibitions.

"Trent," I called while he rubbed my feet after we had walked for miles, touring and enjoying the city for hours.

"Yes," he answered and leaned in to give me a quick kiss.

"I want you to answer honestly when I ask you this."

His smile froze, and seriousness flashed from his unblinking eyes.

"Would you date me? If we exchanged numbers, would you abandon your serial one-night-stand status and just date me?"

The long pause spoke for him. The idea of giving up what he was accustomed to wouldn't be an easy decision, especially not for someone he'd only known for two days.

"I honestly don't believe I'm ready for a long-term, monogamous relationship. The longest I've lasted has been twenty-five, maybe thirty days, and it ended horribly. I'd rather not drag this out."

I nodded, forcing a smile like his words hadn't shredded my heart into a thousand pieces. I prayed he'd be kind enough not to turn my question around on me. I would have said yes to him in a heartbeat.

I hadn't given up on my design career when the harsh blows of rejection had struck me down. Something inside wouldn't allow me to give up on Trent so easily, either. I aimed a finger at the nightstand.

"I'm leaving my number there, and it will be up to you whether you want to take it or not."

A flicker of something stirred in his gaze, but he glanced at where I placed my number and nodded before I was able to decode what had flashed in his eyes.

"Are you thinking about tomorrow? Are you ready to go back home and resume your normal routine?" His questions were meant to drive us away from the subject of prolonging a moment that was only meant to be a speck of light in time.

A hard swallow dislodged my reply to his questions from my throat.

"Yes. This weekend..." a sad but genuine smile surfaced this time, "this weekend was amazing."

And I don't want us to end here.

"But I'm ready to go back home. I have so many design ideas I want to work on."

He took my hand, kissing the back of it.

"It's going to be okay, you know. I was your first...fling, and we extended it. Time is a bitch, and it makes separating difficult, but we've got this," he said. His words were expressed with enough positive energy to be convincing, but they made me question if he was persuading me or both of us.

It didn't occur to me until we were climbing into bed for the last time that he'd confessed to doing this hundreds of times. Therefore, he was probably used to getting the most from short periods of time with women. Additionally, he'd always have the next time. His next hook-up.

As for me, he would be my one and only, and I couldn't help feeling like I was allowing something special to walk right out of my life.

***

Trent

My heart, mind, and body were engaged in this exchange with Callie. She knew how to wrap herself around every part of me so damn good, it was like she was inhaling me, and I loved every minute of it.

She wouldn't complain about it, but I acknowledged the pull of her stiff muscles and the soreness that would edge out in quick winces from the endless, insatiable sex we'd overindulged in. My energy levels had reached a critical low, but we'd managed to give each other the sexual satisfaction we craved.

Time was running out. I wanted more of it, but I wasn't selfish enough to prolong our situation. I'd rather end this, especially with her, on a positive note.

"Tell me more about yourself, Callie. You've heard a lot about me these last few nights. I want to know more about you."

"Does it matter? Richmond is a big enough city that after tonight, we'll probably never see each other again."

I knew that I'd hurt her feelings when I lied to her face and told her I wouldn't date her. Truth was, I wanted nothing more. However, I didn't believe I had what it took to have a successful relationship, and if I didn't believe in myself, I was doomed to fail us, to fail *her*.

"I'd love to hear about you regardless of what's to come. Do you have any sisters or brothers? What about your parents? What made you want to be a designer? What were you like in high school?"

Her low chuckle sounded genuine.

"Sounds like you want the whole diary of Callie Dayana Hendrix, not the breezed-over speed dating version."

I squeezed her to my chest, my lips brushing the top of her hair. "I'd like to know all that you are willing to tell me."

I already knew about her meeting her friends and college, and at a certain point in her younger life, she'd ended up in foster care, but I wanted to know more details.

"I'll go with the easy stuff first. I grew up in Richmond with my mom. We were poor but our needs were met. In school, I was what most would consider a nerd: glasses, quiet, and in love with books. I joined a lot of clubs in school. The yearbook club, 4-H, and the

Newspaper club. My favorite was the book club because it allowed me to indulge in my favorite pastime, which was..."

"...Reading," I chimed, smiling.

"If I wasn't picking up a book, it was magazines. And I didn't like the educational books either. I wanted the adult romance books I had no business reading. I was reading about clit licking and cum dripping before I fully understood what they truly meant."

I chuckled, picturing her with pigtails hiding under a desk with an erotic book.

"Looking back on it now, I didn't join the clubs because I was interested in them. I joined because it was the easiest way to guarantee that I'd have friends. Someone to talk to throughout the day, someone to sit with at lunch. I feared being that kid who sat alone, that no one would talk to because I wasn't cool, witty, outspoken, or popular."

I propped my hand behind my head, genuinely interested in her past. I wanted to know what had shaped her into such a hardworking, lovable woman.

"Fast forward a few years, and things took a turn, but not for the worse, more like a linear path. My father left my mother when I was a baby, and when I was ten, she, for reasons I never knew, also decided to leave. I was left with my grandmother. She, like my mother, wasn't a nurturing woman, and although my granny beat my butt from time to time, I didn't consider it abuse because every other kid I knew got the same."

This made me think about my own mother taking a belt to my bad ass. I agreed with Callie. I didn't believe it was abuse either because I'd done too many things to deserve those beatings.

"My granny was an alcoholic. I didn't know what that was back then. All I knew was what people called her and that she drank every day. On the days she couldn't get alcohol, I stayed clear of her. A few years after moving in with her, at fifty-six, she died of liver failure. No one could find my mother or any of my grandmother's family, so she ended up being cremated by the city, and I was placed into a foster home. At first, I didn't see it that way, but later, I considered myself one of the lucky ones. I ended up with decent enough people who were raising five other foster children. There was never enough time devoted to each kid, but I was already used to not having a nurturing bond with the adults in my life."

She paused and glanced up.

"Am I boring you to tears yet?"

"No. You're not boring me at all. Keep going, please," I urged.

"Design started with me cutting up my clothes to make outfits for my dolls when I was staying with my grandmother. I didn't like that they were stuck wearing the same clothes every day, so I took it upon myself to start making them some. I can't even remember how many butt whippings I caught for cutting up my own clothes. At one point, my grandmother hid my dolls away for months. Then, design was reintroduced to me in a more elaborate way in my high school home economics class."

She paused at a memory, her face fixed in a smile that enticed mine.

"After cooking class came sewing. The teacher first introduced the idea of us making our clothes. She taught us the basics of creating and designing patterns. We chose the material, and she let us loose to sew the pieces together, and I was hooked. I'd found my calling," she laughed. "I even begged my foster parents for a cheap sewing machine from the thrift store."

She chuckled at the memories I sensed swirling around in her head.

"In high school, the kids teased the hell out of me because I started wearing the clothes I'd made. I didn't care what they had to say. I was proud of what I made, and besides, my skin was thick and tough by then, so words didn't bother me."

Her smile surfaced and widened at whatever crossed her mind.

"I met Charlene and Dayton in college. We connected so fast it was like we'd always known each other. I stuck with design, even when it felt like it would never go anywhere. Making clothes made me happy, but reaching my goals was a slow process. I ended up working all types of jobs I didn't want until my designs began to pay off. Fast forward a lot of years later, and here I am, at twenty-nine, finally designing and making clothing for three living dolls that are worshiped by millions."

"Here you are," I stated. "I am proud of you for persevering with what made you the happiest. Lots of people, myself included, would probably have given up."

"Thank you," she stretched her neck to place a sweet kiss against my cheek. "I appreciate that."

Silence spilled over us, and eventually, sleep claimed us because the next thing I knew, my eyes snapped open. Callie was on her stomach, her feet tossed across one of my legs while her body lay sprawled in the opposite direction.

The covers rested right above the beautiful globes of her ass. Damn, she had a sexy ass.

The red digital numbers were flashing: 2:15 a.m. It was officially the next day and the last I would see her.

Tucking my hands behind my head, I allowed my thoughts to consume me. Yesterday, she asked if I'd be interested in us being a couple. I'd shut the idea down without giving my thoughts the time they needed.

Although I'd been asked that question many times, I'd never had to think about how to answer it. I was always sure I didn't want anything other than sex.

My gaze became transfixed on Callie's sleeping form. She was the only woman who made me think, *what if?*

I enjoyed her company. We could talk for hours and never run out of things to say to one another. She listened to me rant on and on about what I wanted from life and praised me for having the drive to better myself.

No other woman was interested enough in me to even ask what I wanted. None knew that I had accomplished more than being the guy who fulfilled their sexual fantasy.

My head shook involuntarily. What the hell was I thinking? I couldn't have a relationship, especially not with Callie. She was too good a woman to be stuck with me. I could already picture myself fucking shit up.

While I was thinking about it, I may as well keep it real. Callie was out of my damn league. What could I bring to her table? She was accomplished on a level that I never even pictured for myself. What would make someone like her want to stay?

Not a damned thing.

She deserved better than a stripper. She deserved better than a guy who'd turned the habit of one-night stands into his own personal dating system. What if we got together, and I couldn't stop my bad habits? She wasn't the kind of woman you fucked around on. She wasn't the kind that deserved...*me*. I would bring her value down.

I eased up, dragging my leg from under hers. Her labored breathing continued even as the bed creaked under my shifting weight. I couldn't do that to her. She may be upset with me for a while, but she would eventually understand that I'd done her a favor.

My roaming gaze landed on her phone number, which she had scribbled on the hotel's stationery. Standing at the bedside table, I reached for the number but stopped myself. My hand balled into a tight fist.

If I took that number, I *would* call her. I'd want to be with her. I'd want to soak up all that genuine care she exuded. I'd want to rest in the nurturing spirit she possessed that I believed could wrap around my own restless spirit like a warm blanket.

"I can't," I muttered under my breath. I can't take from her without anything substantial to give back.

After standing above her for what felt like an hour, I finally made up my mind. Leaving her was about to rip out a part of me, but I believed it was the most unselfish decision I've ever made.

"Goodbye, Callie. I love you," I mouthed before I turned and walked away.

Chapter Six

Trent

A year later.

The long shower refreshed me after a hard workout, but my stomach roared noisily, telling a gut-clenching story of my ravenous state. The gym my friends and I frequented wasn't as big and elaborate as the new-age ones popping up around Richmond, but this one wasn't always jammed-packed. We enjoyed the peace that came with keeping our membership here.

Atlas drew my attention, his voice animated, retelling one of his secret rendezvous. He was the oldest of the three of us and the only one who'd been married. His attitude about women sprang from his train-wrecked marriage, and I had no desire to be trapped or responsible for someone else's feelings or their lives. Besides, my job didn't inspire women to take my desires seriously, so there was never a reason to let things get that far.

I concentrated on Atlas' words. He was only talking about his new fling to me and Ransome because the relationship was over now. He never disclosed anything until he knew he was done with the woman, whether it lasted a day, a week, or his max of two weeks.

Unlike me and Atlas, Ransome was the hopeless romantic of our group. As a result, he'd allowed women to take an ax to his feelings more times than I cared to remember. However, this was the first time he'd allowed Atlas and me to see the hurt. He'd gone and caught feelings for a woman who was fresh out of a ten-year relationship.

Out of nowhere, the woman Ransome was dating, Charlene, announced that she was taking her ex back. Now, he moped around, looking sad and pathetic. It was like watching a lost, big-eyed puppy whose only goal in life was to find someone to love.

Atlas and I had given him the 'I told you so' speech, but what did he expect? Women didn't take us seriously. The stereotypes and stigmas attached to the job left many women unable to separate the two.

I felt sorry for Ransome. His head was in another hemisphere. My brows pinched while taking him in fully. His gaze fixed on his open locker. He was truly into Charlene, and for her to dump him out of the blue to take her ex back was fucked up. We didn't have the most desirable jobs, but that didn't mean we could be treated like dirt and expected to take the abuse.

***

An hour later.

Three quick snaps of my fingers in front of Ransome's face got his attention.

"You there, man?"

He blinked out of his daze to see what I wanted before turning his attention to where I aimed my finger.

"We're here."

We'd left our practice session at the club, climbed into Atlas' car, and driven to one of our favorite spots to get something to eat. I doubted Ransome noticed that we'd even left the building.

Once we stepped into the restaurant and were seated, I tossed around ideas in my head for how to pep Ransome up. I sure as shit wasn't hooking him up with another woman. I even contemplated calling Charlene myself and demanding she tell me why she dumped him, even if it meant me stealing her number from Ransome's phone.

A little shiver danced up my spine, making the hairs on my arms stand. I lifted my arm and glanced down at my pebbled flesh.

What the hell?

What was causing me to react like this?

Ransome, though he sat in front of me, had zoned out, his attention captured by something behind me. I leaned to the side and glanced back to see what he stared at so intently, and my heart turned several cartwheels in my chest at the sight.

Callie.

My mouth dropped open, and it took me a few lingering seconds to close it. I'd seen her weeks ago at the club with Charlene and a group of other ladies, and it had taken an army of universal soldiers to keep me backstage and away from her, but I kept my distance.

When I took the stage, she had conveniently walked away. Here she was again. In the same space as me. This time, there wasn't a stage or screaming women stopping me from approaching her. I sat at our table as quiet as Ransome, drooling over the memory of our time together a year ago.

My time with her, though presented as a one-night stand, turned out to be one of the best weekends of my life. Regret was a constant companion since walking away from her, reminding me that Callie was the one I let get away.

I often lied to myself, my internal arguments convincing enough to make me believe I was saving her from my inability to be in a long-term monogamous relationship since I'd never had one. However, something deep in my gut kept telling me that Callie was worth me at least trying. Now, I doubt she cared to remember me. If she did, she probably wouldn't speak to me.

Leave them while they are sleeping. That was my signature departure move, but leaving Callie hadn't been easy. I'd walked away three times only to turn back and stop myself from shaking her awake. I'd forced myself to step out of the door, knowing I had no way to get back in unless I woke Callie up. Even then, I stood outside the hotel room door, ready to knock. But, like the coward I was, the idea of being with one woman terrified me more than the lonely nights that were a constant in my life.

I waved a hand in front of Ransome's face. He was staring so hard at those women that I was afraid he'd scare them off.

"Earth to Ransome. Earth to Ransome. Ransome, you there?"

This was the second time I'd had to snap him out of the cloud of sadness surrounding him.

"Aren't they your girlfriend's friends? Kind of hard to forget a group of women that damn fine," I asked, already knowing the answer.

Ransome waved when the ladies acknowledged him with smiles. Atlas sat next to me, twisting his neck and body around to get a look. My eyes were glued to Callie, but she placed her gaze everywhere except on me.

"Aren't you going to invite them to sit with us? Just because their friend dumped you, doesn't mean you need to blackball the rest of us," Atlas said, his expectant gaze boring into Ransome.

"Hell, no! Not so you two hounds can sink your teeth into them or play your little catch-and-release games," he replied.

The nerve of him. He was conveniently forgetting that he'd allowed his dick to plow through the lines waiting to get their turn with him. Now that Charlene was in his system, he was acting holier-than-thou. His ass wasn't innocent.

"Come on, man. They're hot. And not cheesy or slutty hot either. They are classy and hot, like that friend that dumped you. I have to admit, if you have to get dumped, it may as well be by a classy ass hot chick like that," Atlas teased.

He teased Ransome, but his eyeballs were sparkling with intrigue. His interest rested on one of the women at that table, and I prayed it wasn't Callie.

He flashed Ransome pleading eyes, begging him to invite the ladies to our table. Ransome picked up his plate and stood.

What was he doing?

"Excuse me, gentlemen," he said before he walked away, leaving us sitting at the table. I didn't protest his actions because the longer I sat there, the more I feared facing Callie.

Atlas, on the other hand, couldn't hide his hurt feelings. "You ass," he hissed after Ransome.

"Ladies, if you don't mind. May I please join you?" Ransome asked humbly.

Damn, she is beautiful, I thought, eyeballing Callie smiling up at Ransome before sliding over to allow him to sit on her side of the booth. She wasn't sporting her glasses today, but in the short time I'd had to get to know her, I'd never decided which I liked more, her with or without them.

"Your friends are going to hurt themselves over there," Callie's friend stated, looking over at me and Atlas as we damn near broke our necks to look back at them. The war in my head had ended, allowing me to reach a conclusion about getting closer to Callie. There was nothing wrong with gauging her reaction when she saw me up close. Would she be upset? Had she moved on with ease like nothing had ever happened between us?

I scooted over, bumping Atlas' leg for him to stand. He got the hint and led the march toward the lady's table.

"Mind if we join you, ladies?" Atlas asked.

Thankfully, one of us had manners. My one-track mind was planning to sit at their table without even asking.

"Sure," the friend answered with a huge smile plastered on her face.

"I'm Dayton, and that's Callie," she introduced.

Callie waved and managed a sincere smile. She didn't appear upset, but she did look conflicted, especially with me sitting at the same table as her. Our gazes met across the table.

Me and Atlas sat next to Dayton at her side of the booth with Atlas in the middle.

A cordial conversation kept us going, but the vibe at the table remained tense. Atlas finally broke through the thick silence settling in on us, commenting on Callie's top. She eagerly shared that she'd made the top herself and designed clothing for a living, and it launched them into a conversation about, of all things, fashion.

The pulse in my neck jumped, adding to the tension in my tight shoulders. Atlas wasn't flirting with Callie, but

I didn't like that he was talking to her and laughing with her. He even knew things about fashion that kept their conversation going on and on.

When I could take no more, I stood.

"I need to get out of here. I have something to do. It was nice meeting you," I blurted out, avoiding Callie's gaze. Maybe some fresh air would cool the heat radiating in my face and the dominating tension using my body for a punching bag. I still wanted Callie and it was my own damn fault I didn't have her.

Chapter Seven

Callie

The vivid memories made a year breeze by like it had all occurred a day ago.

"One night," I repeated. *"One night,"* he reiterated.

The words reverberated in my head, a haunting echo: sad, sweet, and tangy. We'd made the pact without knowing how our time together would affect us.

Trenten Pierce.

Thinking his name saddened me, but it brought on an easy smile at the same time. Bitter-sweet. Smooth-roughness. Silky-hardness. He was all of those opposing adjectives.

I'd breezed through so many books about one-night stands and loved them all because they were fantasy, something you never dreamed would happen to you in real life. But it did happen to me. Too bad the shit didn't turn out anything like it did in those books. We broke the pact we'd agreed on and turned our one-night into a three-night weekend.

Big mistake.

If I'd walked away with my dignity intact the next morning as I should have, I believe I would have had a great one-night experience to remember on my lonely days. Instead, I'd allowed emotions to settle in deep and manifest into something I didn't want to lose.

Who does that?

Me, the one-night-stand idiot. I'd convinced myself that I could hang on to a fantasy man when the whole point was one night. The fantastic thrill ride was timed, dated, and stamped, *temporary.*

Seeing him again after all this time stirred all kinds of old feelings I assumed had disappeared. They hadn't. They'd only remained dormant, waiting to be reawakened by him. Being near Trent now reminded me that I'd allowed myself to fall for him less than a day after I'd met him, maybe even the same day we met.

Now, he was in my life again by association, and I didn't know how to process what seeing him again was doing to my mental stability. Thankfully, his friend Atlas began talking to me because the awkwardness that swirled around the table was thick enough to slice through.

When he jumped up and left the table, I wanted to go after him, not having a clue what I wanted to say. Now, ten minutes after Trent's departure, I couldn't stop thinking about him.

After checking to make sure Dayton would be okay with being left alone with Atlas, I decided to leave myself. Instead of heading to my car, I took a detour to the little park a few blocks away. I needed to clear my head.

A deep, chest-lifting inhale allowed me to take in the fresh air. I loved that I lived in a modest enough area that allowed me to experience a city rush and still breathe fresh air. The mid-June sun didn't flex its muscles today as a light breeze licked my skin.

Unseen birds chirped while the breeze swept leaves from the trees and scattered them along the area. In the distance, waist-high grass connected thick patches of trees that swayed like they were giving a performance for the crowd. Parents were busy chasing kite-flying, bubble-blowing, and playground-storming kids. A few couples scattered blankets along the grass and relaxed lazily under the warm blanket of the sun. I took in the scene and appreciated this live movie with its impromptu script.

I sat on a bench facing the small, man-made lake, lifting my head to the sun to soak up some vitamin D. Why did I have to see *him* again? Now it would take all types of mental gymnastics to keep him from invading my memories.

"How have you been, Callie?"

I jumped, placing my hand across my chest as my head shot up.

Speak of the devil, and he appears, I thought, glancing up at the handsome one standing above me. He'd made me jump this same way the first time he'd introduced himself to me.

"I've been fine," I answered, hoping my words didn't sound clipped. I didn't want him to think that his presence affected me in the least.

"May I?" he asked, aiming his hand at the open spot on the bench beside me. I glanced down briefly before my head snapped back up to him.

"Did you follow me?"

He smiled.

"No. I was standing outside the building taking a call when I saw you come out. "

"Oh," I said before gesturing toward the open spot.

We sat in the deep pockets of our silence, searching for something to say to each other, I suppose.

"It's nice seeing you again, Callie."

I didn't reply, as I didn't know what to say.

"I hate goodbyes, so I took the coward's way out and left before you woke up. I apologize for doing that."

"Thank you," I said, glancing up to meet his waiting eyes. The apology was unexpected but accepted.

"This year will be my last year dancing. I've earned my degrees and decided to invest in my own business, with seasoned partners, of course."

My smile deepened. "I'm truly happy for you. You had a dream, and you're making it come true. And you did it within your timeline, right?"

He nodded. "Yes. I'm thankful that dancing allowed me to chase one of my dreams. Now, it's all on me to make sure I work my ass off to take it where I want it to go."

He nudged me playfully.

"I'm not the only one who pursued a dream and made it come true. You were already making it happen, but I saw you on television. I also read the article about you in Impression Magazine."

My head jerked back at his admission. Had he been secretly keeping tabs on me? I'd be lying if I said I didn't peek at his social media pages every once in a while.

"You read that article?"

He nodded, and another awkward silence fell between us.

"What's it like touring with a famous group?"

"It can get chaotic, especially now that Twisted Minds have won several renowned awards and their sophomore album went platinum. The crowds have quadrupled since the first time I traveled with them, and their fanbase is expanding by the day. It's at the point now where many of the fans attempt to go through me to get to them. You'd be surprised how often I'm offered money for a face-to-face with the group."

He stared, smiling at me, making the little quiver in my stomach increase its gnawing pace.

"I love it, though," I continued. "Being able to do what I love and have the world see my designs displayed on stages around the country. Sometimes, I have to pinch myself to make sure it's all real."

"You are talented and hardworking, and your work speaks for itself," he complimented.

My cheeks warmed. "Thank you."

The seconds ticked by and stretched on endlessly.

"Well.."

"I..."

We muttered at the same time.

"You go," he said.

"I better get going. I have a long day ahead of me tomorrow," I lied.

Tomorrow was one of my rare days off to enjoy. But, for a reason I didn't understand, I didn't want him to know that.

"Enjoy the rest of your day," he said.

We stood, but neither of us moved. We smiled awkwardly at each other, me aiming a thumb across my shoulder and him nodding. The intense hold he took of my senses was like nothing I'd ever experienced. The same gravitational anomaly happened the first time we met, and even after a year, the chemistry or whatever it was luring me to him was just as strong. I didn't want to want him, but dammit, I did, and it wasn't all physical either.

"Yeah," I said, aiming my finger across my shoulder for the hundredth time before I spun on my heels and took off.

Don't look back.

Don't you do it.

Don't you dare look back.

I kept chanting the phrases to myself.

When my head did turn to glance across my shoulder on its own accord, my gaze collided with his. He hadn't moved an inch. The forced smile on his face didn't make it to his eyes and was laced with *regret.*

Was I seeing what I wanted to see, like I wanted to believe we could have more than a weekend? I shook off the question. Tricking myself into believing things I couldn't physically touch was not a mistake I was making again.

Chapter Eight

Trent

Two weeks later.

I fingered my tie, wanting to yank it from my neck but opting to straighten it instead. I hated wearing suits but knew I would stick out like neon lights in a pitch-black sky if I dressed down for this fancy fashion show.

These types of events weren't my cup of tea unless I was one of the models in the show. However, I was particularly interested in this one because Callie's designs were the main attraction.

This didn't count as stalking her. At least, that's what I kept telling myself. I had a legitimate excuse for my attendance if I happened to run into her. I would lie with a straight face about networking to book more modeling gigs.

The truth was, I rarely sought out gigs. My agency would find them, and I usually got back-to-back bookings before I hit my seasonal dry spells.

I'd also brought a date as extra backup. A woman I'd bumped into while I was exiting the gym three hours ago. Now that I was here, I began to question myself and my motives. I wanted Callie—there was no doubt about that, and the only thing holding me back was the uncertainty of her response. Why the hell had I brought a date when it would only fuel Callie's decision to stay clear of me?

Callie.

My breath caught, and my heart rate made its presence known. The pulse points in my neck and temples jumped, the beats echoing in my ear.

A pair of thick-rimmed dark-framed glasses added an astute and sexy vibe to her appearance. The stylish frames drew my attention to her face, at which point I became lost, admiring the smooth, delicate lines of her lips, and her jawline. Her luminescent skin appeared as smooth as butter. With just a flick of those long, seductive lashes, her eyes ensnared me while her lips enticed me to lick mine.

I don't know how the woman did it. Visually stunning, she brought life to whatever accessories she wore or created with her own hands.

That dress. Her elegant movement made the teal silk wave and flow as if fighting the wind for the privilege of touching her skin. She offered her full right shoulder as a gift while the left rested inside a loose sleeve. Moon-shaped cut-outs under her ample breasts gave you just enough of a teasing peek to make you stare. That I knew what was under that dress made me breathless.

A radiating confidence drove her movement across the room, eyes following along like they were reading a mysterious fantasy. My tongue traveled along my bottom lip.

Beautiful.

"Are you staring at her hard enough?" my date asked, glaring at me, acting like the pig I was being. I dropped my gaze and didn't reply. There was nothing to say— she'd caught me fair and square staring at my...

Callie wasn't *my* anything. What was I saying? We'd had three nights together.

"Would you like anything to drink?" I asked my date, distracting myself from the only thing in the room I wanted to see.

"Yes. Please. Get me a Martini—two olives."

"Be right back," I replied, scanning the crowd for Callie before I took the first step.

Five minutes later, and the bartender was bringing us our drinks. What bartender anywhere made drinks that damn fast? I'd counted on him being slow so I'd have time to scope out the scene for a woman I had no business checking out. A woman I had walked away from without so much as a goodbye. It was a mistake I prayed I could take back nearly every night for a year.

Now, I would have to get back to *my date*. Why did I bring a date? Was I unconsciously hoping to make Callie jealous? My intentions were to enjoy her show and be supportive without making her feel uncomfortable. However, it was only now that I acknowledged that, date or no date, me being here was making a statement all by itself. On my way back to my date, I was spilling our drinks. I felt the liquid sloshing over the top of the glass but it didn't stop me from keeping a keen eye out for Callie.

"Thank you," Mari exclaimed, taking the drink and sipping from it greedily.

Something in the back of my mind yelled, *look*. When I did, there she was again, heading my way with a beaming smile on her face. Her eyes danced back and forth between me and my date, who hadn't noticed her yet.

When my date finally did look up, she caught me staring again. I sensed the woman's eyes burning a hole in the side of my face. I dropped my head, but I refused to lower my eyes for fear I'd miss seeing what I'd come here to see in the first place.

A quick burst of nervous energy raced through me, making my heart rate kick up a few paces.

Callie was the only woman who could make me lose my center of gravity and not care about replanting myself on solid ground. She made me see through a lens of infinite passion. Her touch molded, shaped, and created dreams. Her voice eased away every torturous idea. Was it a good or bad thing that someone had that much power over you without even knowing it?

"Hello," she greeted, her voice delicate and soothing. She eyed me and my date, her smile inviting and sincere.

"Hello," I replied, pausing so long that my date nudged me in the side.

"Mari, this is my friend, Callie. Callie, my date, Mari," I finally made the introduction.

Callie stuck out her hand, and Mari took it with a smile so fake that I was surprised her lips didn't fall off her face.

"Nice to meet you," Callie told her.

"Likewise," Mari returned, looking down her nose at Callie. I didn't like it and fought not to put her in her place.

"How do you two know each other?" Mari asked since we stood there surrounded by the odd tension circling our group.

"We had a weekend fling. We knew what it was and were adults enough to move on and still remain cordial to each other afterward."

Unprepared for Callie's candor, I cleared my throat.

"I knew it. Knew it based on the way he kept staring at you when you walked in," Mari stated. She shoved the drink she'd nearly finished back into my hand, some of the cool liquid spilling over the edge and narrowly missing my pant leg. The eye roll she leveled on me caused me to ease back a notch.

"You know what, I'm going to save myself the trouble and do my own thing tonight. You may have been adults about your fling ending, but you two are definitely not over. I'm out," Mari said, walking away and throwing up two fingers over her right shoulder before letting one finger drop.

I stood in place, swallowing hard from being thrown off guard for the second time in less than five minutes. Women these days were not playing games with us. They would either get what they wanted from us or move the hell on like Mari just did.

Uncertainty stirred. Should I apologize for what just happened? Was it wrong of me to be glad that Mari left?

"Was she right? Do we still have unfinished business?" Callie asked, her brows pinched.

"I..."

"Callie. My Callie," a loud male voice shouted, cutting me off. The man the voice belonged to approached with one stiff brow lifted, looking down on me like I was the trash stuck under his shoe. He was a few inches taller than me, which put him at least six-four. His dark chocolate skin glistened against the light, and his teeth sparkled. He must have been one of the models in her show.

His Callie?

The little frown on her face indicated that she didn't want to be *his* anything. He walked up behind Callie and slid his arms around her waist. She cringed before plastering a smile on her face, faker than the one Mari had flashed a moment ago.

"Trent, this is Donni. Donni, my friend, Trent," she introduced us. I noticed she hadn't given him the same spill about our weekend fling. Was she protecting his ego or mine? Neither of us bothered to reach out a hand to each other.

Raw male tension choked the space surrounding us. My gaze dropped to where his hand rested on her waist.

Her voice was the only thing that cracked the burning rage building within me.

"We need to get going. It was nice seeing you, Trent," Callie announced, turning quickly and out of Donni's arms.

"You too," I replied, my focus zeroed in on her while ignoring the intoxicating level of useless possessiveness being displayed.

Donni, her soon-to-be ex, tossed me a cocked gaze and turned to follow her. I squinted after them, praying she would turn back or at least look back and give me a little flash of hope.

My silent call was answered. She tossed a glance over her right shoulder. Our gazes locked long enough for a smile to tease the edges of my lips.

Mari had been right. Callie and I were far from being done with each other.

To prove the point even further, my intentions were to go home after Callie stepped away with Donni. However, here I was, forty-five minutes later, still eye-stalking her.

Her show was a phenomenal success that people continued to buzz about. Their praise caused pride to swell within me for her. My eyes bucked at the sight of Callie with that Donni character.

For reasons I couldn't name, I refused to let her out of my sight. He hadn't been one of the models, but I did notice how random people kept walking up to him, asking to take selfies. He must have carried some type of celebrity status.

Callie didn't seem all that interested in being with him as she entertained guests and networked. The entire time he was glued to her side, he never once picked up on the subtle hints that she wanted to be left alone.

Case in point, her removing his hand from the small of her back or leg couldn't have been a more obvious clue that she didn't want him near her. Now, my body was knotted with tension due to my concern for her safety with this guy.

Thirty minutes later my concern began to turn into full-blown panic. She wasn't acting right. She kept lulling to the side on the couch they lounged on, as though she could barely keep her head up. Although the asshole kept supplying her with drinks, she was only taking small sips from each one, so I'd venture to say she wasn't drunk. I hoped that motherfucker hadn't drugged her. Certain men couldn't resist the sick lure to do nefarious shit to unsuspecting women, even when it was unnecessary.

At first, I silently observed her with him from afar, but now I was a fucking wide-angle lens, zooming in on every move he made. When he helped her stand, there was no doubt something was wrong.

I followed them, not caring anymore how I was acting toward a woman that wasn't mine. There was no way I was letting him take her anywhere when she could hardly hold up her head and needed assistance with walking. The crowd kept me from catching up to them.

My heart hammered, my breaths rushed out, quick and sharp. Where the hell were they?

"Get out of the damn way," I muttered, shoving a guy making his move on a woman who was more interested in the woman standing next to her than him.

Donni and Callie walked clumsily through the front door while I pushed past the crowd. I hope he'd valet parked. Otherwise, a taxi could whisk them away, and I'd never forgive myself if something happened to her.

"Thank fuck," I muttered to myself when I spotted them waiting on the passenger side of the sleek black Lexus the valet drove up in. Donni reached for the door, his other hand gripping Callie's arm.

Just as he was about to shove her into the passenger side, I gripped her free arm.

She lifted her head, her eyes dazed enough for me to know that she was under the influence of something. I didn't give a shit if she'd volunteered to drink it, snort it, or smoke it. She wasn't going anywhere but with me in her condition.

"I'm not letting her go anywhere with you. She's under the influence, and I know her well enough to know that she's not some pill popper who would be this careless."

"Who the fuck are you? Captain save a hoe? Take your fucking hand off my woman before I call security. Do you know who the fuck you're talking to?"

I got in his face, snarling so angrily, he flinched and eased his head back.

"Ask her who she would rather go with," I bit out, placing a possessive hand around her waist and dragging her closer.

"My Callie," Donni called to her.

She lifted her head, slower this time.

"Do you want to go home with me or that chump over there?"

She nodded but with no understanding of what she was saying yes to.

"Callie, sweetheart, I'm going to take you home and make sure you're safe," I assured her. Again, she nodded. This time, recognition flashed in her gaze.

"Trent," she called out, her voice barely registering.

I fixed my eyes on the meaty hand clamped around Callie's arm.

"You can either let go of her arm, or I'll detach that motherfucker from your body and leave it in this parking lot."

He lifted his hand then, no doubt seeing the dangerous gleam I knew was playing out in my eyes.

"This bitch is fine, but I can get this level of fine any time I want," he said, snatching his arm away. He cursed under his breath, staring daggers at me while he walked around his car.

I walked Callie closer to the building to safety in case Donni wanted to do something stupid.

The screech of tires and the shriek of black the car left in its wake was his, *fuck you*, to us. I honestly didn't give a shit what he did as long as it wasn't directed at Callie.

Once we stood closer to the entrance of the building near other pedestrians, I cupped one of her cheeks and forced her to look up and acknowledge me.

"Callie, baby, look at me."

She did, flashing me a set of unfocused eyes.

"I'm going to take you home and make sure you're okay."

She nodded.

"Do you know what he gave you? Was it just drinks?"

She shrugged.

"Just drinks," she slurred. "I feel funny."

"Do you need to go to the doctor?"

She shook her head.

"Sleep. I need to sleep."

Saying the word had her eyes closing on their own.

"Don't worry. I'll take care of you. Let's get you home," I told her, walking us back toward the valet booth for my car.

Chapter Nine

Trent

I couldn't keep my eyes off her. Callie Hendrix was in my bed. *My bed.* This was nothing like when we'd first met, but the sight of her sleeping so peacefully a year later kept me right there next to her.

This woman was special, whether she knew it or not. She was the only one who'd inspired me to desire something beyond a fling.

Although I hadn't followed through on the relationship I wanted to pursue with Callie then, I was grateful for the time we'd shared. It meant something to me. She was the highlight of my day when life kicked my ass. She was the one I had stupidly let get away, and if life gave me a second chance with her, I wasn't going to waste it.

Now, we were here, at a crossroads with curves so slick and bendy that I didn't know what to think. One minute, I would talk myself into proposing that we give each other another shot. The next minute, I would talk myself out of it. And I couldn't forget about her ex. He'd committed a crime against her, and I still couldn't help wondering if she'd been considering taking him back.

What if she didn't want me now? What if she did? What if I wasn't ready and did something to hurt her if we did pursue a relationship?

However twisted up my thoughts were, there was one thing I was certain of, I would take care of her, no matter how long she needed it or wanted it. I would also follow up on the asshole who'd drugged her, so he wouldn't continue to do that to other unsuspecting women.

There was no justification for a man who chose to drug a woman to take advantage of her. It was a criminal act, and men like him belonged in jail.

***

The next morning.

She stirred, releasing a light groan while coming out of the peaceful somber she'd retreated to. With her forearm slung over her head, she peeked up at me through one squinted eye.

"Trent?"

She struggled to sit up, her shaky elbow pushing into the mattress while the veins in her neck strained with the tension on her face. Her efforts didn't pay off because she collapsed back against the pillows.

"Careful," I coaxed.

Concern tightened my forehead while I stepped around the bed to assist her.

"How? What happened? I was ..."

She was still confused. Her eyes searching to calm the internal chaos disrupting her mind. I eased onto the bed next to her, placing a careful hand on her arm and the other on her lower back.

She eased up again, slower this time, with my assistance. Her free hand delicately stroked her forehead to ease the ache I knew pounded in her head. Unfortunately, I knew how she felt as, in the past, I had experienced the aftermath of several depressant drugs that I had used recreationally.

Once she was sitting up steadily, I fluffed a pillow behind her back before turning to the bedside table to take up a bottle of water.

"Here, drink as much of this as you can."

I ignored her hand and placed the bottled water up to her mouth. She allowed me to help her drink. I had three other bottles sitting there waiting for her.

"What do you remember about last night?" I asked her.

She stared straight ahead, dragging her mind for details before she lifted her gaze to me.

"I remember seeing you. Then, I was talking to my ex, Donni, and like he always does when he sees me, he attempts to convince me to take him back. I turned him down, but he said that we were friends and could at least have a drink together."

She paused and stared down until more memories lit her gaze.

"A decent conversation sprang up between us, and next thing I knew, we're talking about going back to his place."

She shook her head, her face squinting into a deep frown. "That can't be right. We aren't hostile toward each other, but I wouldn't go back to his place—"

She continued working out the details of last night in her mind.

"Damn," she whispered. "Was I that desperate that I was about to go running off with my ex?" she murmured the question to herself, contemplating her actions. Her fingers slid across her hair that I had pulled back into a messy ponytail.

"You weren't that desperate, but apparently he was," I told her, the comment regaining her attention.

She stared up then, one brow lifted in anticipation of what I had to say.

"I believe he drugged you, Callie. I wasn't trying to be in your business, but the scene didn't look right. It didn't feel right. When I got a good look into your eyes, I knew without a doubt something was wrong. I got you away from him. Brought you back here so you could sleep it off."

Silence permeated the room. She sat, staring at nothing, her lips parted. The news had her fidgety and picking at the covers. Her left leg jumped while wide-eyed fear flashed in her gaze.

"He drugged me?" It sounded like a question. Her eyes begged me to tell her it was a lie, but I couldn't.

"That son-of-a-bitch drugged me." This time, it was a statement. It was an acknowledgment she found great difficulty in believing, based on how she kept shaking her head like she was trying to make the news go away.

"You think you know someone, but no matter how much time passes, how much you've shared with them, how much you've sacrificed to make them happy, you never truly know a person," she said, the distaste in her tone spilling over every strained word.

I placed a tender hand atop hers.

"I assumed I'd have a tough time convincing you that he'd done that to you, especially after you confirmed that he was your ex."

The sorrow in her watery gaze tore at my heart.

"When we were together, he was a serial cheater. I forgave him more times than I should have. One of the girls he cheated with claimed he'd drugged her. And I chose to believe him when he said he didn't. Believed the lie he'd told me about the girl being a gold digger trying to get a payoff from him. Now, I know better—know that he is capable of anything."

She slipped back into her own head, muttering under her breath with a few curse words thrown into the jumble of words.

"Are you going to be okay?"

She shook her head. "No. I'm not okay."

I squeezed my hand around hers. Relief washed over me when she allowed me to hold on to it while giving mine a weak squeeze.

"All this time, he could have been doing that to so many women. And like a fool, I believed *him*."

"We need to go to the authorities," I stated.

Thankfully, she nodded, and a fresh sheen of tears glistened in her eyes.

"I have to. If he could do that to me, someone he dated for a year, think about what he'd do to someone he doesn't know at all."

Her shoulders dropped at the notion. I hated the next idea that crawled into my head. *What if that wasn't the first time he'd drugged her?*

"I honestly don't know if going to the authorities will do any good, but I have to do something," her words were weighted with heavy concern.

My forehead furrowed.

"You don't think it will do any good? Why?"

"He has celebrity status because he's internet famous. On top of that, his family owns half the state and has influence over things like law enforcement and businesses—you name it. Money talks."

I shook my head. "If this guy is that well connected and he and his family are rolling in money like that, then why not just pay women who are willing to do what he wants instead of drugging them? I don't understand."

Her shoulders lifted high and fell fast.

"I don't know. He may get a thrill from knowing that he's doing something wrong and getting away with it. Some people are wired that way."

My fingers tightened around hers to reclaim her attention.

"Can I ask you something?"

She nodded, and I could tell by the way she bit into her lip and searched the empty space that she was figuring out what to do next.

"Were you with him last night because you were considering taking him back?"

"No," she answered quickly. "Taking him back has never been something I've considered after we parted."

I contemplated my next questions carefully, but my curiosity spurred me to continue.

"I mean no offense when I ask this, but didn't you sense anything suspicious while you were dating him? That he was keeping things from you or sensed that something may have been off with him?"

Her gaze fell away from mine, and she released a defeated sigh.

"I did. I'd heard all sorts of rumors but decided I'd give him the benefit of the doubt and take his word for it. He claimed people were jealous and driving a wedge between us, especially when women would call me with cheating allegations. At the time, he was believable, so I put blinders on and didn't pay much attention to all the little things that were happening right under my nose. The late nights, the phone calls at all hours, the odd looks from certain women when we would go out. I let myself get pulled into his lies so deeply that I didn't know what was true anymore."

I squeezed her hand, lifted and kissed the back, allowing my lips to linger against her warm skin.

"I didn't mean that you should have known anything or should have detective-like skills. I'm guilty of playing a few of those stupid ego-driven games myself. Some men are just dicks. We make it our mission to get what we want without considering that we are playing with the lives of women, many of whom may want something real. I had a lot of growing up to do to break that type of behavior. I'm not Mr. Perfect, and you know this, but I am honest and upfront."

She nodded and gave me a quick, sad smile but didn't reply. We fell into a companionable silence before she moved again.

"I better get going. I appreciate you taking care of me last night. I'll drive myself to the police station later to file a complaint on him. "

She released my hand to peel back the covers. The emptiness the action left behind had me staring at our broken connection.

"Are you sure you're okay to walk? You can stay here for as long as you need to."

"I'm okay. I just want to go home, shower, and climb into my bed."

She stood to her feet but didn't move right away. She reached out, I believed to take my hand but then dropped her hand quickly.

We stared at each other for an odd, lingering moment.

"Thank you for taking care of me. Thank you for getting me away from him."

"No problem," I replied, aiming a thumb across my shoulder. "I'll grab my keys so I can drive you home."

I didn't want her to go, but I had enough common sense to know not to pressure her. She needed the space and alone time to process all that had occurred last night.

***

The first half of the drive to her apartment after she gave me the address was filled with a tense silence. There was a discussion that needed to be had. One that I believe we were avoiding. The subject of us. Was this the right time for me to bring up us?

Minutes later, I helped her out of the car and walked her up to her door. The thick silence between us was a third wheel, rolling along and strongly representing our avoidance. Once the door was opened, we turned toward each other and leaned in for an awkward hug. She reached low, and I went high. We switched for a better angle only to get our arms tangled.

"My bad."

"Sorry."

We stepped back, and I turned quickly, took a few steps, and stopped abruptly with a noisy foot shuffle. When I glanced across my shoulder, she remained in the same place, watching me walk away again.

I turned and marched back, my forehead pinched tight with all that I held back.

"Can we talk?"

She nodded, her head motioning quickly. Was she relieved that I'd turned around?

Ushering with her hand, she turned to allow me to enter her place first.

I stepped through the doorway and glanced around quickly, smiling at not only where I was but how representative this place was of her. The quilt thrown over the back of her couch appeared to have been put together with a piece of every known fabric. The lamp atop a stylish metal end table displayed a lampshade that was undoubtedly one of Callie's creations. I took the matching loveseat adjacent to her comfortable grey-brown microfiber couch.

Callie chose to sit next to me on the loveseat. Her leg brushed against mine when she sat. The innocent touch had me sucking in a calming breath.

A year away from her and the draw to her remained strong, letting me know the cords connecting us had never been severed. Her presence excited me, calmed me, and got me all riled up in no particular order.

This was not the time for my blood to start heating up. I called for calm to lay claim over my restless soul. We had serious topics to discuss.

I started with a part of what was being left unsaid.

"The time we spent together last year. It was one of the best of my life. Our time left its mark on me, making me acknowledge that it wasn't a random event and that the connection we shared was genuine and lasting."

Her gaze penetrated deeper than the surface of my eyes as she remained silent, assessing me. The quiet heightened my unease and kept me on edge. She was the only woman who could make me lose my normal confidence and humble myself. She made me feel. Everything.

I needed to tell her what had been bothering me from the moment I stupidly walked out of her life. When I saw her in that restaurant and sat so close, the ideas that swirled around in my head had increased to the tenth power. I wanted to express to her that after a year, I had a strong desire to apply action her suggestion that we give each other more time. I wanted her to know that I missed her. Missed the sound of her laughter. Her voice. The way she made me feel special.

"I wanted more time with you last year. I wanted to give you the extra time you asked for, but I didn't want to start a relationship with someone like you and not be able to deliver on it. You deserved someone better than me, someone who could give you everything you needed and wanted, and I…" I shrugged. "I didn't think that I had that type of devotion and love inside me."

"Someone like me?" she asked.

I nodded, my face warm. Was I…*blushing?* Had I just allowed an unusual sense of shyness to course through me?

"When I say someone like you, I mean that you're one of those women a man doesn't walk away from. You're beautiful, smart, and hardworking. Kind of soft-spoken, but not a pushover. You're like the perfect blend of the things most men are looking for in a woman, and if a man doesn't come to you with the best of intentions, they shouldn't even be in your presence."

She listened intently, her gaze bouncing back and forth between my lips and my eyes.

"I believed at the time that I didn't have enough to offer. I honestly didn't think I could be the type of man who could add balance or anything substantial to your well-planned, hard-earned, and successful life."

I was unable to read what was on her face. Her eyes searched mine like she was determining if my words were genuine.

"You're accomplished. Successful. Hardworking. You've achieved many of your goals. What about now? Do you feel the same way you did then? That you can't measure up to what *you* projected my expectations of the man I want in my life should be?" she asked, her brow lifted high in anticipation of my answer.

There was a swarm of relentless thoughts in my head, each waging war on my mental focus. She probably didn't think that I understood what she was saying, but I was listening. I had made the decision for her last year, thinking I knew best what she wanted.

"It's only been a year, but I've grown more as a man. I stopped holding women accountable for the way they treated me, realizing it was up to me to demand the respect I sought. I stopped with all the one-night flings, accepting that it was my way of getting back at women for what wasn't their fault in the first place. I long ago outgrew stripping and stuck around for the fast-paced money, and I will be retiring soon. I've done some deep soul-searching, and although I don't know if I can be the man I know I'd need to be for a woman as special as you, I've accepted that I'd damn well like to give it my best shot."

There it was again. Silence. The long stretch of silence that fell between us after my statements threatened to consume me. My pulse jumped, my breaths got away from me, and my head began to spin. She tilted her head upward, processing every word I'd spoken.

The blessed sound of her voice after such a long pause, whether she was about to knife me in the heart or not, eased some of my tension.

"The time we spent together was unforgettable. I wanted so much more, but I knew it wasn't fair of me to ask when I knew what we had agreed to. I've thought about us a lot through the year, always wondering, *what if* we had tried? What if we worked and could make each other happy for a longer period of time, no matter how long it lasted? Another weekend, a week, a month, I'd have taken any amount of time, as long as it was more. That's how much I enjoyed being with you."

She released a long-winded sigh.

"So many what ifs. So many, I wished. I was so upset with you for leaving that it took me a few months to understand in my head *why* you felt the need to leave the way you did."

The sound of our accelerated breathing filled the space, cutting into the empty silence I hated.

"I don't know what might have happened if you had stayed. We could have come to the decision to just walk away. But, like you, the time we did spend together left an impression that's followed me all the way up to this point. That precious time all those months ago made me want to try back then, and it makes me want to try now. What you did for me last night..."

The idea of what happened to her last night was like ice water being poured over both of us. It wasn't something we could ignore. We had to deal with it, and the sooner, the better. I laid my open palm on her lap, and she placed her warm, soft hand inside mine.

"Let's try together." I lifted her hand and placed a delicate kiss on the back.

I gave a little tug, dragging her closer. She reciprocated the kiss, her lips pressed against the back of my hand now. She kept her mouth there, allowing me to feel her smile.

"I'd like that. I'd like to try," she whispered.

"Hot damn," I called to the ceiling, my voice booming through her living room.

"So, it's official. We are a couple? I'm your man, and you're my woman?"

She giggled, the sound filled with the same joy I'd heard from her a year ago.

"I like the sound of that. You're my man, and I'm your woman," she repeated, testing the statement.

I brought her hand back to my lips, smacking kisses to the back of it repeatedly to express the level of joy coursing through me. Fear knifed through me with no mercy, but I was determined and already praying that I could make this beautiful woman happy and keep her that way.

I wasn't a religious man and rarely ever prayed, but this time, one came to me in the midst of our prolonged hug.

Lord, please keep the demons of our past out of our future. Please fight the devils that may come for us on our behalf. Please forgive me my past stupidity and allow me to call on the common sense I know I possess to do everything in my power to love, support, and make Callie happy. Amen.

Chapter Ten

Trent

Callie glanced up at me, peeking through one eye.

"Why do I feel so awkward all of a sudden?"

"You just made an important decision about your life. You made it sound like it was an easy one to make, but I know that it wasn't. It's scary. It's life-impacting. It's humbling. It's difficult to explain. I feel awkward too, but in a weird sort of comfortable way."

Her big, bright smile let me know that she understood my long-winded approach to agreeing with her.

"There you are," she smiled her words, soft and warm like the care resting in her gaze. "This is the part of you that is so genuine and good, expressive, but most importantly, thoughtful. When you first told me what you did for a living, I didn't believe it, not even after you assumed you had convinced me. It wasn't until after I saw you dance a few weeks ago that your words truly took root."

She thought I'd lied to her about being a stripper? Did she think the story was an elaborate lie so she'd not want to see me again after one night?

"You being a dancer made me understand more why you thought that you couldn't enter a relationship with me. However, there was a part of me that didn't—that never cared about your job. It was you, the part of yourself you never let anyone else see or enjoy, the part I believed you protect at all costs. Until you decided to give me a peek at the real you in New York. And that was all it took for me to see past everything surrounding you."

My brows lifted.

"You saw all of that in me?"

She nodded. Her light stroke to the back of my hand sent my eyes to our connection.

"Will you stay with me tonight?"

My lips parted, but nothing came out. "*Say yes*," a voice in my head demanded. I nodded before forcing my voice box to work.

"Yes. I'd like that."

My hand closed around hers, squeezing lightly before tugging her closer. We closed the last feet of the distance separating us, our energy swirling and tightening the space around us. We stopped right before our lips met. Our eyes searched, our hands working and squeezing wherever they landed.

My leg jumped to contain the surges of energy coursing through me, most of them settling in my belly. These charged emotions. This high. Callie was the only one who could make me feel this way. I believed it was the reason I'd never stopped thinking about her after all this time.

We moved as one, our lips meeting and lingering in a breathless flow of emotions and passion. Sparks lit up and ignited all over me. This captivating world we were transported to belonged only to us.

I moaned against her lips, instantly addicted to the sensations riding me, marking me, uniting my spirit with hers. She responded to my urgent kisses, my fumbling hands, and my breathy moans by deepening our kiss.

A few breaths later, she backed off. Her eyes spoke to me, revealing that she was being consumed by the same heat that had erupted within me.

"I need to wash last night off of me," she said, her words a warm whisper. She stood but didn't step away. She reached out a hand for mine.

"Will you join me? I'm a little weak and may need some help."

"It will be my honor to help you clean off the drama of last night or any other night that comes to mind."

My chuckle turned into a boyish giggle as she dragged me behind her. Who the hell was I with this woman? If my friends saw me now, they would taunt me to the end of time, but I wouldn't give a shit.

Callie reached blindly into the shower, turning on the water while her lips continued caressing mine. Reluctantly, our lips parted when I reached down to finish my job of getting her pants off. My eyes trailed down.

Legs.

Hips.

Body.

I was on autopilot at this point, reacting to her sexually possessive vibes and committing every caress to memory.

"Callie," I called out between kisses and my fumbling hands. She didn't answer right away. She was too busy stripping off my shirt.

One of my eager hands tested the weight of her full breasts, encased in black lace. The woman was sexy-slim but thick in all the right places.

Damn!

"Yes," she finally answered, slipping my zipper down and hooking her fingers in the belt loops of my jeans.

"My intentions were to be a gentleman, to talk, and to make sure you were okay."

"Were?" she questioned, pinpointing the key word in my statement while taking my pants down until I kicked them the rest of the way off.

I slid my hand up her soft round thighs and lifted, hiking her up and around my waist. With us in only our underwear, the press of her warm skin against mine was a form of foreplay all on its own.

"I missed you," I whispered, not sounding like myself, but meaning the words because they were for her.

"I missed you too," she replied, gifting me with a smile.

Her breathing kicked up a notch when I squeezed her cushiony cheeks and slipped my tongue into her mouth.

I walked us into the shower, the hot water making us gasp as it beat against our skin before adding a relaxing vibe to our runaway desires. I didn't stop moving until she was pressed into the wet slippery wall, my hips pushing into her inner thighs, my dick starving for a taste of her pussy.

"I can't wait. Are you on..."

"Yes!" she answered, cutting off my question, already knowing what I wanted to know.

"Good."

Slipping her wet panties to the side, I inched back, aligning us, but I didn't move right away. I had to commit this to memory, us, wet, hot, and filled with a restless need for each other. Nothing else existed—nothing else mattered.

I thrust into her, the stroke hard and long against her slippery-tight and welcoming depth. When my shaft slammed all the way into the warm, sweet, resisting force of her clenching walls, it nearly took me out.

A lightning strike of hot pleasure shot up and down my spine and weakened my knees. She was my wildest fucking dream come true. I paused, my eyes shut tight and my body shaking to ward off my need to come.

Shit!

Callie didn't move, but her pussy had no mercy on me. The tight slickness wrapped around my dick pulsed harder and grew wetter. With my lack of movement and my low, throaty groans, I sensed that Callie knew what my problem was without me uttering a word.

In my defense, I hadn't had sex since that weekend a year ago. It was like my dick had been put on pause, and my desire to screw other women had been sucked into a black hole. The idea of me not wanting to have sex fucked up my head at first, but over time, it allowed me to put things in perspective where my relationship with women was concerned.

Despite my long stretch of celibacy, I still let the guys at the club believe whatever they wanted about me, and I even told lies to keep the ruse going. Therefore, my reputation for being a notorious one-night lover never diminished.

I moved, concentrating on pleasing the woman who'd taken up residence in my head for a year. Callie had no idea that her face and body were what had consumed me, mentally and physically, when I considered being with other women.

The year before I met Callie, I plowed through women like I was in a race. The year after I met her, I may as well have been a eunuch. No woman after Callie would do and it wasn't something I believed I could talk to my friends about. I didn't believe they would understand, although Ransome probably would now.

I would meet a woman, and the desire I had built up would fizzle out. Their voices were never right. Their hair was all wrong. Their skin tone was off. Their bodies didn't turn me on enough to go through the act. They weren't Callie.

"Trent," she whispered, her eyes closed. Water drizzled down her body as she waved and twirled against my long, deep, and slow thrusts. My fingers dug in deeper, tightening the grip on her hips and thighs to help ground me against the overflowing pleasure racing through me.

"So good," she moaned, her gaze keeping a tight grip on mine before her eyes fluttered back closed.

The sight of us, water pelting and drizzling down our skin, and the way we sensually waved against one another was intoxicating. Her soaked black panties clung to her beautiful, blushed-kissed brown skin. The endless flow of our desire competed with the hot drizzle that tickled our skin and licked its way down only to be replaced by more. If there was a heaven on earth, this was it.

"Callie. Fuck!" I cried harshly, my head falling back while I shuttered in ecstasy. I wasn't going to last long, not with the way her sweet pussy was gripping my dick. And the way she kept crying my name.

"Trent. Oh. Trent."

Somehow, the slippery grip of her arms around my neck remained while I controlled her legs around my waist and the entrenching depth of each rotating grind. So deep, so mesmerizing.

Any second now, I would lose my shit. It was too good. I switched to a waving rhythm, in and out of her, picking up the pace with each thrust.

Too fast.

I was moving too fast. The waves of lust, the hot flashes of our bodies slapping together to create this magical moment. It was impossible to stop myself, especially when she kept saying...

"Trent, right there. Oh baby, right there."

Her body shuttered, her closed eyes tightened, and her lips parted with silent cries. I understood every reaction because I was there with her, ready to let whatever force overpowering us take control. The first tight squeezes of her pussy muscles around my dick took me out.

"Fuck, baby. Pussy so fucking good," I said. I knew I was saying those words, but I couldn't hear myself. I was coming so hard I had to lock my knees to keep us from slipping.

I shook uncontrollably, but there was nothing my body could do to contain the explosion of ecstasy that overpowered me.

I floated away on a cloud outside this reality, but I never let go of the notion that Callie was right there with me. We soaked up every last drop of the delicious thrill until the hot water beating against us assisted in bringing us back to reality.

"Damn, that was... amazing," I said, smiling and nuzzling her neck with my wet nose. Her legs slipped off my waist and down mine. I let my hand slide up her body until I found her bra hooks and popped them open.

"Let's get clean and..."

"Continue," she finished with a seductive smile.

Chapter Eleven

Callie

Trent took his time washing me, spreading the lather over my body with slow and deliberate strokes. When his soapy hand slid between my legs, I swallowed a moan and fought not to close my eyes to the sensations he coaxed out of me.

My sex life wasn't an active or exciting one, not before Trent. It was more like occasional events spurred by the layer of dust I'd allow to settle on my lady parts. I'd always been that way, which was the reason many of my boyfriends had dumped me.

I didn't put out enough for them. Was it that the men I dated didn't know how to hype up my libido, or had it been me?

This was a battle I'd been having with myself since the day I decided to have sex for the first time at the age of twenty-four. I was a late bloomer for most things in my life, and sex wasn't excluded. I'd waited all that time to have sex with my then-boyfriend of a year, only to end up throwing up on him because the experience had been so bad. The traumatic events of that night, I'm sure, were the catalyst for my sluggish sex life.

However, my weekend with Trent had been a turning point in my sex life. Being with him just felt right. With him, I wanted the sex, and so far, he was the only man who could make me want it badly and often.

Before Trent, going months without sex didn't faze me. After him, the urges ravaged me and tortured me so badly that masturbation became my new norm.

No one I met ever scratched my itch like he did. My desire peeked out and turned up its nose whenever I even attempted to force a sexual connection with someone else.

Like now, I squeezed my thighs together, trapping his hand between my legs. The move put a teasing smile on his face.

"You're hot for me again, already, and so fucking wet. If we weren't in this shower, my hand would be soaked with your warm juices."

He whispered this in my ear while moving his hand so the tip of one of his fingers strummed my clit and sent a shiver of pleasure up my spine.

He reached down, picked up the soap, and squeezed some into his hand. If he kept this up, I would come again soon, but not yet. I wanted to be wrapped around his magnificent dick or leaking on his meticulously giving tongue when I did. I soaped up my hands, unable to resist letting them slide over his velvety soft skin that splayed over hard, flexing muscles.

My soapy hand movements had him biting his lips and doing a weak-kneed dance that told me his heat level was rising along with mine.

His dick lifted and bobbed before stopping to aim at my stomach. It drove home the point of where it was aiming to go. Trent was big, and impressive with a reach potential to cause damage if he didn't know what he was doing.

"That's good enough, baby. We are clean enough," he said, taking the soap from my hand and sitting it on the little granite shelf carved into the wall behind us.

He turned so the water rinsed him and sprinkled on my face, and then he turned me for my rinse. I committed

this moment and stunning view to memory because...*damn.*

We didn't play the same game drying off as we had
climbing into the shower. I tossed Trent a towel from my
cabinet, and we brushed the fabric carelessly over our
bodies while eye-fucking the shit out of each other.

Half my body remained damp. I hadn't bothered with
lotion or anything. All I had time to do was swipe deodor-
ant under my arms before he jerked it from my hand and
swiped it under his. The sight caused me to giggle, but it
didn't stop me from turning to walk into my bedroom.

I gasped when a quick turn spun me off balance. Trent
had caught me right before I got to the bed, snatched me
by the waist and arm, and spun me into his hard body.

As soon as our bodies smacked, his mouth was on
mine, and his hands gripped my ass. My gasp was kissed
away by desire and licked away by his tongue.

My pussy throbbed at the pressure of his straining
erection pressing against my stomach and working its way
down with each move we made. He spun me again, turning me so fast my wet, shoulder-length natural hair
slapped the opposite side of my face. I gasped at the speed
at which the top half of me was forced down to the mattress, my face colliding with the soft comforter.

Two hard licks to my ass had me crying out against
the unmerciful sting, intensified by the moisture that still
clung to my cheeks. His damp feet nudged at the inside of
mine, calling my attention long enough for me to assist
and spread my legs wider.

What I expected and what I got were to different ex-
tremes as he dropped to his knees and planted his face
between the back of my legs and his mouth on my pussy
within seconds.

"Oh damn," I cried out at the press of his mouth, his lips, and his wickedly expressive tongue dipping in and out of me and licking my wet folds with a vigorous hunger that amped up my passion. I was getting high off the man's tongue.

"Trent," I called out, unable to help twirling my pussy against his mouth. He responded with faster tongue strokes, the tip pressing against my clit and flicking with enough pressure too...

"Fuck. Oh! You..."

I came hard and fast, and he didn't ease up on his delicious tongue stroking until I heaved against the mattress and ran from him. I'd escaped the sweet torture, for now.

"You can run from my tongue all you want, but you are not going to be able to run from this," he said, gripping his dick and shaking it at me while I glanced back. He was so lewd and confident. And I liked it. I liked it a lot.

"Spread your legs. Wide. Don't matter if you're on your back or your knees—the choice is yours."

The command had me reacting like I was a soldier in training. I did what I was told even as the remnants of the orgasm continued to flutter around in my system. This man made me insatiable in a way I didn't recognize. I wanted to see him pleasuring me, so I positioned myself on my back, my legs spreadeagled.

He did more than climb in and connect our body parts. He used his lips on my stomach, his tongue on my nipples, his masterful eyes all over me, and his fingers to drag me deeper into his world.

His sensual caresses left goosebumps on my skin. I savored the way his tongue raked up the topside of my quivering thigh and admired the way his eyes soaked in every part of me that called their attention.

He made me believe I was the sexiest woman on the planet and he was the only man capable of bestowing the special gift. Easing the ache, scratching the itch, making love to my soul.

Once our bodies were flesh-to-flesh, and he lay between my legs, I allowed my fingers to tease along his shoulders, back, and neck until I had my arms clamped around him. He licked up the side of my neck while his body began to move in a short, rotating rhythm. There was no reaching between us to position his dick. He taunted me, allowing his hardness to press into me while our movements worked it down to the area I wanted him most.

When the head slipped across my sensitive clit and swiped my wet lips, I gasped so hard that I was surprised I hadn't swallowed my teeth. He eased back and forth, his movement so slight and the sensation driving me to the point of madness. I was beyond ready and was about to yell it when...

"Oh. Shit. Trent!"

He thrust into me, spreading me open and going so deep that the head stroked my soul. He worked my body, and his deep ins and outs made me swivel under him, eager for the full impact of his sex.

"You okay?" I think he asked, but I was too busy trying to breathe. I nodded but was so consumed by the grinding pleasures riding me that I lost my ability to think or react.

My focus zeroed in on where we were connected. I managed to glance down and was rewarded with a view of us: the swirling intensity of our damp brown and beige skin, the rhythmic flow of our bodies, and the intensity that set our minds on fire and made our bodies burn in the flames of delicious desire.

"Trent. My. Oh. I'm." I breathed out a mix of words that didn't make sense. He kissed me hard, crushing our lips together before he slipped his tongue into my mouth. The kiss was the best kind of distraction, giving a different type of pleasure that allowed all the other sensations I was experiencing to stretch out like it would go on forever.

His unyielding length pressed and dragged along my inner walls, reaching a depth that produced an ache so sweet that my body was on the verge of merging with his. I gripped him hard, locking my arms around him. Somehow, I managed to lock my legs around him, too, which impeded his movement but kept him buried deep. He knew what I wanted and found a way to keep his grinding movements flowing enough to massage my inner walls with a hypnotic flow.

"Oh. Oh. Trent." It was the closest thing to words that I could push out. The flow of the impacting orgasm ripped me apart in the best possible way, causing my head to lean like that of an addict who'd had her fix after suffering the effects of withdrawal. I was so far gone I didn't know if I shook, shivered, quivered, or if there was even a difference.

"Callie."

My name was being called from a distance.

"Are you with me?"

I nodded, but my brain hadn't fully latched on to the present state of my reality.

Trent had sent me clean into another dimension, blowing my mind and setting me aflame with all that was good. Although we were no longer connected, my lady parts continued to clench and release, hanging on to the pulse of the most intense orgasm I'd ever experienced. My fingers and toes tingled. My body hummed. My bones were gradually rebuilding because I'm sure they had melted.

"I'm..." I struggled to answer him. "I'm here," I managed while a lazy smile eased across my lips.

And just like that, I was his again after a year of yearning. A year of praying and hoping. Trent, with his sweet words and calming way, had lured me back into his world. I wanted to be his, and needed him to be mine. I prayed with all I had that we lasted longer than a few days this time.

Chapter Twelve

Trent

Callie.

I had Callie on the brain. When someone engaged me or asked me a question, they had to repeat it because my head was wrapped around the only woman to capture my attention. She was beautiful, but that wasn't why she kept me engaged.

Callie had that thing I didn't have a name for that drove me to look past her gorgeous face and banging body. I enjoyed talking to her. I wanted to share my ideas with her. I wanted her opinion on things that mattered to me. And I wanted to know everything she was willing to share about herself.

"Trent, did you hear what I said?" Topaz, the partial owner and head emcee at Quiet Chaos, the club I worked at, waved a hand in front of my face. I was on my way to the dressing room, and she'd stopped me to ask…something.

"No. What did you say?"

"Luca called and said he can't make it tonight. Will you be able to do two sets?"

I nodded. "Yeah. That won't be a problem."

"It will be a problem if your dancing is as scatter-brained as you are now. You're not on that shit, are you?"

My head jerked back like the question packed a physical punch.

"Hell, no! You know me better than that. It was a life-time ago that I've buried twelve feet under."

"Okay," she said, eyeing me with suspicion. I rolled my shoulders and tilted my head left to right to loosen the tension in my neck and shoulders. There was another set of eyes on me, and although I didn't spot him, I knew it was Topez's fiancé.

Anytime I was anywhere near Topez, her lingering boyfriend gawked and gave me the stink eye. If he was that damn insecure, he needed to have a heart-to-heart with his future wife. Topez's bread and butter was managing strippers and co-owning a strip club, which would require her man or life partner to have a certain level of confidence that her current one didn't possess.

"I've got you," I assured when she kept those assessing eyes on me. "I'll see you later." She nodded and returned the smile I flashed her before I stepped away.

I needed to get some rehearsing done as well as figure out what costume I would throw on for my second act before the floodgates of Quiet Chaos opened.

***

An hour and a half later, and after my rehearsal session, the sounds of the crowd filling the club filtered into the dressing room.

"Trent! Trent!"

Hearing my name being shouted jolted me from my Callie haze.

"Yeah. Why the heck are you yelling?"

Atlas' face squinted into a tight knot, his unblinking gaze set on mine.

"Because I've been calling your ass for a straight minute. What the hell is wrong with you?"

He aimed a finger at Ransome before pointing it into his own chest. "Should we be asking *who* is wrong with you instead?"

"I'm fine. Can't a man think?"

Atlas nodded, and I could practically see the sarcasm he was itching to spill oozing from his pores. I continued before he could start in on me.

"We are minutes away from stripping off our clothes and shaking our dicks in front of a bunch of horny ass, dick-grabbing, very strong, and determined women. The noise level in this place alone prevents one from forming a concise thought, much less resonating on one."

Ransome tilted his head, his eyes squinting. He must have recently talked to Charlene because he didn't look like a damn zombie today.

"The only other time I saw you like this was over the woman who you wouldn't let us meet. The one you claimed you wouldn't have minded getting to know. You know, the one you got all sensitive about when we teased you. Have you met someone else?" Ransome asked, his eyes widening and flaring with anticipation while awaiting my response.

I glanced up, assessing him and Atlas. These two men were my best friends. We valued each other's advice and it's why our friendship worked so well. They were the only ones I trusted explicitly. They were the only people I truly believed had my best interest at heart.

"It's the same woman," I blurted out.

Ransome jerked his neck up and pinned his gaze back on mine. Whatever he was searching for inside his locker was forgotten. Atlas took a seat next to me on the bench, his neck lowered to my level, his head tilted in interest.

"Dude, you look too serious right now? What are you saying? What do you mean, it's the same woman?" Ransome asked.

I met his waiting gaze.

"Charlene's friend, Callie. I met her a year ago when I did that modeling gig in New York. She was the designer on set. We agreed to a weekend together and stuck to the agreement, but I never stopped thinking about her. Never stopped thinking that maybe I made a mistake walking away from her."

Ransome scooted closer, his wide eyes searching me for understanding.

"The woman who had you all lovesick last year was Charlene's friend? Callie?" Ransome asked.

Atlas sat staring, assessing me.

I nodded. "That day in the restaurant when we joined you at their table, imagine my surprise when I sat in front of the one woman I actually liked. The one I wanted more time with. The one I never stopped thinking about. Somehow, the planets aligned and put us back in each other's paths. I can't make the same mistake I made the first time."

Atlas waved his hand in front of my face, but I ignored the smart comment I sensed he was about to release.

"It looks like Trent, even sounds like him, but alien tech is generations ahead of ours," Atlas said, staring like he didn't know me at all.

"You two are looking at me like I've been abusing small animals all my life or some shit."

"Charlene's friend?" Ransome asked again, unable to hide the tension around his eyes. I pointed a finger at Ransome. "Yes, Charlene's friend, Callie." I turned the same finger on Atlas. "I'm not a fucking alien. I'm me. I can be more than a man-whore-prick. Cordial, polite, and accommodating. Those are a few of the words the women I've dated have associated with me."

Pride danced along with my words while Ransome and Atlas lifted disagreeing brows at me.

"I've also heard asshole and pile of shit, but I'll let you stick to the good adjectives," Atlas blurted, unwilling to let me have *some* joy.

The frown on Ransome's face managed to grow deeper.

"You get what you want from women a time or two and dump them on their asses. You being nice to them makes the situation that much worse because you lead them to believe they have a good guy they can be with long-term when you know you're not going to stick around," Atlas pointed out, continuing his rant.

He had a point, but Callie was special. I rolled my eyes at Atlas, who sat there like he wasn't the master of speed dating.

"All this coming from a man who sees women in secret, and only after you've dumped them do you spill the details of your secret rendezvous to us like you're in a therapy session."

"I make sure they know what they are going to get and for how long. By the time we go our separate ways, there are no hard feelings."

"How do you know?" Ransome asked Atlas. "You delete all contacts and ghost them after you leave. You've never shown any of them where you live. Hell, you even lie to them and tell them you have no family."

I stifled a chuckle. Outside ears would think we were a bunch of rabid animals. Ransome was the tamest of us all. He possessed that pretty boy look that automatically got him labeled a playboy. Still, truthfully, he was the one who'd wanted a relationship from the start.

Atlas was the secret playboy. The most you would see is him leaving with a woman and never hearing from her again, not even at the club. What was he telling them to make them stay away and not bother him anymore?

It wasn't uncommon for women to chase my ass down at shopping centers or at the club like I'd proposed to them.

"This is not about me," Atlas pointed out, luring me from my runaway thoughts. He shook a finger in my direction. "This is about you and the fashion model."

"Designer. Callie's a high fashion designer," I corrected.

"Same difference," Atlas stated nonchalantly. "Have you ever seen a designer who didn't look like they couldn't model all the clothes they made?"

He did have a point, and Callie was gorgeous, and her body...

"Like I said, we met in New York last year. We started a conversation, and that was it. We hit it off. Had our time until it ran out. Now, here I am, a year later, and my best friend is dating her best friend. I spotted her at the club the night they came in, and weeks later, I walked over and sat at a table in front of her. You can't tell me the universe isn't giving me a sign."

Ransome lifted a brow before nodding. Atlas pursed his lips but didn't comment. It wasn't that he didn't believe in faith—it was that he was having a hard time believing that I was serious about pursuing a relationship with one woman.

"Charlene means everything to me. If you hurt her friend, it means you hurt her, and we are going to have a problem. So, if you two decide to break things off, please do it respectfully and with class. Please," he begged.

"So, does this mean you and Charlene are back together?" I asked. His plea hadn't gone unnoticed. I prayed they were back together so he could stop looking so damn sad.

"There's still hope for us," was all he said before his eyes dropped to the floor.

Ransome rarely begged for anything, so hearing him beg me on behalf of a woman he barely knew so as to not hurt her, was eye-opening. He was not playing when it came to Charlene.

A smile crept across my lips. I was proud of Ransome. He'd never given up on finding his one, and I prayed that he and Charlene officially got back together.

"I promise you, brother, I'll do everything in my power to make sure Callie doesn't get hurt," I promised. Ransome glanced up and nodded. Atlas stared through his long lashes at me, unwilling to believe I was serious about someone. I would show him better than I could tell him.

***

Arm and legs heavy with fatigue, breathing taking longer than usual to level out, stomach muscles twitching—at twenty-eight, I felt every second of doing this job. I had entered my veteran status according to the stripping industry.

It felt like I needed to limp the way my left calf muscle kept jumping. I sent up a quick prayer after every dance, grateful that nothing was twisted or broken. All that thrusting and popping and lifting and twisting had me imitating a washed-up sixty-year-old wrestler who'd just been suplexed off the top rope. Thankfully, in less than a year, I would be financially healthy enough to set myself free of this job for good.

The night was cool for June, in contrast to how sweltering it had been earlier today. Though it wasn't windy, a stabbing chill swept through the air, causing my shoulders to hike. I glanced around the near-empty parking lot while adjusting the strap of my bag on my arm.

The five lights spread throughout the parking lot sat on highly arched telephone poles. The lights flickered, looking like giant eyes winking at me in contrast to the lower city lights. A few cars hummed by in the distance, the head and tail lights zipping through the dark street.

I aimed my key fob across the lot at my Black Mercedes CLS 53, smiling at the sight of it because it was bought and paid for. My hand flew up to shield my eyes when the bright lights of an approaching vehicle screeched rapidly from the darkness.

Where the hell had it come from? Why was it heading straight for me?

"What the fuck?" I muttered, cupping my forehead to block the light, and picked up my pace to my car since I was closer to it than the building.

This motherfucker didn't look like they were going to stop. The engine's growl grew louder by the second. Were they going to fucking run me over?

"Fuuck!" I yelled before I took up a slow jog.

I'm not going to make it.

Fuck that, I'm going to make it.

Only feet away, the small SUV wailed like the sound of a demanding voice telling me to get the fuck out of the way. Dropping my gym bag, I threw myself through the air, landing just out of reach of the revving vehicle's front end.

Who the hell?

There was no way they didn't see me. They were coming right at me.

My heart knocked on my chest plate so hard that the beats pounded in my ears, making them twitch. My tennis shoes scratched up pebbles at my attempt to back away and stand at the same time.

The driver hit the brakes, and the vehicle came to an abrupt stop before the reverse lights illuminated, joining the red glow of the tail lights.

Was I asleep? Surely I wasn't in the parking lot of my place of employment with someone threatening to take my life?

Had I finally pissed off a woman I'd dated bad enough for her to make an attempt on my life?

The tires screeched when the car backed up as fast as it had sped into the parking lot. I took off in a mad dash toward my car.

After snatching my passenger side door open, I hopped in and slammed the door shut. Before I could get a good look, the car came to a screeching stop. The driver whipped it around so that the headlights were aimed in my direction again.

It took off, aiming for the passenger side of my car. I slung myself across the center console in an attempt to get into the driver's seat, only to get my long legs tangled up in the cramped space between the seat and the dash.

A glance back across my shoulder and my life flashed before my eyes. Callie made an appearance, and I focused on an image of her face as the light closed in on me.

The car, again, came to a screeching stop. This time, less than a foot away from ramming my passenger side door. Those high beams had me blinking, and although the incident had put the fear of God in me, I did my best to see if I at least knew the car or could spot the driver.

The vehicle moved, backing away before stopping and turning toward the parking lot exit. It took off, and I had the presence of mind to memorize their license plate number, only to find that there was nothing displayed on the back of the car. My harsh breaths livened up the inside of my car.

My phone.

Fuck.

Had I dropped my phone?

Thank God, I thought, snatching it from the passenger seat where it must have fallen from my pocket. No longer seeing the car, I sat restlessly, doing my best to regroup by dragging in calming breaths.

Once I calmed enough to think straight, I needed to decide whether or not I would report this incident.

My gym bag.

How far back had I dropped it? Turning in the seat to gauge where it, but the darkness was preventing me from seeing anything other than shadows.

Another glance in the direction the vehicle had gone showed the coast was clear. However, it didn't mean anything as I hadn't seen where the vehicle had come from in the first place. I gripped the handle to my door, easing it open before I stuck my first leg out. My eyes remained on the entrance into the parking lot while I swung the rest of my body from the car.

Leaving my door wide open, I ran back to the spot where I'd dropped my bag. Where the hell was it? I glanced back at the entrance of the parking lot.

"Motherfucking son-of-a-bitch!" I cursed into the night at the top of my lungs. I didn't have to worry about the vehicle returning because they had gotten what they wanted.

"I've been jacked," I muttered, releasing my frustration by punching into the air.

I had worked at this location of Quiet Chaos for nearly four years and had never had so much as anyone look at me sideways—now this shit.

And the most fucked up shit about it was that they had gotten away with my pay for the night. Forty-one hundred dollars in cash. Thankfully, I'd maintained possession of my phone and my wallet. There was no use in calling the police. They didn't like us, the environment we worked in, or how we made our money. Therefore, them helping me track down who'd just robbed me was never going to happen. I was better off hiring a detective on my own.

I'd had serious plans for that money. It was for the weekend getaway I wanted to talk Callie into going on once her schedule cleared up.

Damn!

I returned to my car, closed the door and locked it before heading back into the building to warn the few remaining inside of the incident. There was someone on the loose bold enough to jack us in our own parking lot.

Chapter Thirteen

Trent

Three days later.

"We would like to call this beautiful woman to the stage. She's been dressing us for two years now, and we can't take all these compliments on our attire without giving her the flowers she deserves. Callie D., come on up here," Jinx, a member of the group Twisted Minds, announced, calling Callie out.

Callie didn't acknowledge it, but she was becoming a star that shone in her own light. Designing for a famous group helped, but her clothing drew a different type of attention to the group as well. The group called her Callie D., the stage name she used whenever she was spotlighted on television and social media. I believe I was one of a few who knew the D stood for Dayana.

"Damn!" I muttered to my empty living room. I couldn't get Callie out of my head and seeing her on television being called out for her skills made pride flare within me.

"That's my woman. And damn, she's fine," I said, grinning to myself.

Callie commanded attention whether she intended to or not. Even sitting in my living room watching the Major Hits awards show, I noticed brows lifting in interest and smiles creeping across curious faces.

"She's taken," I shouted at the television when Shark Finn, the famous rapper, hopped up to help her up the stage steps when she clearly didn't need assistance.

"You better take your hands off my woman. I don't care what kind of street creds you're claiming," I muttered at the screen.

Was this how it would be? Would I be competing against men who could give Callie anything she wanted? What was I saying? She could already provide for herself. Was I good enough for her?

Stop this shit! I reprimanded myself. This was the same shit that crept into my head a year ago and caused me to make one of the stupidest mistakes of my life.

My woman was winning in life, and based on that glow on her face, she was winning internally as well. Callie had chosen me. Now, I would have to learn how to handle her being around all of those celebrities.

This was my reality check. The few women I'd dated had to deal with a constant swarm of women at the club clambering for my attention. Callie was already dealing with it with class and grace. I was getting a serious dose of what Callie had to accept about my job. If she could do it, I could do it, even though the people I was in competition with were famous superstars.

My head fell into my palm, even in the midst of my own pep talk. This was the kind of pressure that could drive a man wild.

How the fuck was I going to wrap my head around this shit?

Callie's short, sweet speech won her a thunderous applause. However, her sleek, black, body-hugging dress, which I'd been privileged to see her working on, made its own speech. Her appearance added to the smooth sound of her voice and amplified the amount of attention aimed at her.

Seeing her exit the stage with Twisted Minds made the proud smile on my face grow intense enough to clog my throat.

Me.

Choked up?

What the fuck?

The only other woman I'd ever gotten choked up about was my mother, especially when she reached the milestone of being ten years sober and announced she was starting a non-profit for recovering substance abusers.

My smile dropped, and my head tilted at what my eyes caught on television. Why was the cameraman following Callie and Twisted Minds backstage? Why was he zooming in on Callie's ass? Why the hell was he filming just her now?

I had a problem. A big fucking problem. My ass was *jealous.* And not mildly jealous, either. I wanted to rip out the eyes of anyone who looked at Callie too hard.

Am I tripping? Probably. But I couldn't help myself. She was the first woman I'd ever truly wanted, and I was willing to fight like hell to keep her.

A smile found its way onto my face. Callie was worth it. She was worth me beating someone's ass and going to jail over. And that was exactly what would happen if someone stepped to her wrong.

***

"Hey, you,"

"Hello, my beautiful and famous girlfriend," I called into the phone, my smile so wide it was heavy on my face, beaming at the sound of Callie's voice.

A long silence followed my comment. Had I said something wrong? Then, I remembered, it was the first time I'd addressed her as my girlfriend.

"How have you been? What have you been up to?" she asked.

The hint of glee and enthusiastic way she'd asked the questions said she genuinely wanted to know how I was doing?"

"Well," I dragged out the word. "I got robbed Saturday night in the club's parking lot."

"What? Are you okay? Were you hurt?"

"I'm fine. Nothing but my ego was damaged. They faked an attempt to run me over so I would drop my duffle bag, which was filled with all of the money I made that night. And, like a fool, I dropped the bag and ran for my car. They snatched the bag and took off."

"What did the police say? Are they going to help you get your money back?"

I shook my head, although she couldn't see it. "I didn't bother calling the police. They can't stand us or the establishment and couldn't care less about me losing the money I took my clothes off to earn."

"That's horrible. I see the way women treat some of you guys. I know about the amount of grooming, exercise, and practicing you all have to do. You earned that money fair and square."

"Thank you. I'm glad someone acknowledges that it's not all glory and praise. I try not to complain since it pays my bills and has funded me a decent nest egg, but if I could get a do-over, I would have taken the longer road, gone to school, and worked a crappy job until I reached my goal.

"I believe you were set on the path you were meant to take. You may not know the reasons yet, but they will reveal themselves eventually. I'm glad you're okay. Do you have any idea who it may have been that robbed you?"

"No clue. They were smart enough to remove the license plate from the back of the car, which leads me to believe they've done this before. I warned the rest of the club to beware."

"Be careful. I'm worried about you."

Although I didn't want her to be stressed, it felt good to know that she cared about my well-being.

"Thank you for caring, but I'll be fine. Like I said, only my ego was hurt in the ordeal. The rest of me has moved on to Friday when I get to see you again."

"I can't wait," she added. "I hate to jump on and off, but I have to dress some impatient people who will go on stage naked and call it my latest design if they don't get the clothes directly from my hands."

"Okay. Congratulations on this amazing achievement in your career and life. I am so proud of you, Callie."

"Thank you. That means a lot. I'll see you in a few days. Miss you."

"Miss you too," I replied before hanging up. The grin on my face grew wider at the idea of seeing Callie.

Chapter Fourteen

Callie

"Damn," I muttered, jerking my head around to see if anyone had witnessed me nodding off, although I was likely the last person in the studio.

Tired was an understatement. I had pushed, pulled, and dragged myself through the last four hours of an exhaustingly long day. A shower and sleep consumed my focus. Food wasn't even important at this point.

Thankfully, Twisted Minds were considerate enough to hire a driver for me. I texted him to let him know I was ready to return to the hotel.

The deep breath I sucked in made my chest rise high before I released it, and it gave me enough energy to stand. Once up, I snapped back into autopilot and headed for the exit.

The group had wrapped up an hour ago. I was usually one of the last people to leave after packing and locking up clothing, materials, and accessories we'd used throughout the day.

It was a blessing to be working away from the hustle and bustle of Manhattan. The Long Island location was far enough away from the congestion to allow fresh air to lap at my skin and provided an openness to the atmosphere that I appreciated.

I waited outside the studio we'd used for the photo shoot. The building stood only five stories high. Its exterior was a brownstone style with wide stone steps. Once I stepped out of the front doors, traffic in the distance sounded, and lights twinkled like dancing stars. A loud click sounded when the door automatically locked behind me.

An eerie calm consumed my senses, and the hair on my arms stood. I didn't see my driver or any other vehicles on this quiet street, yet I sensed someone's eyes were on me. Why? I didn't know anyone in this city.

A smile surfaced when the headlights of a car came into view. I stepped down the first three of the five steps and inched closer to the edge of the sidewalk.

This wasn't the black Tahoe that was supposed to pick me up. My face bunched, crushing the smile that had made an appearance.

I stopped, my eyes pinned on the black Mercedes SUV that crept up. Had my assigned driver switched vehicles and not let me know?

The SUV stopped in the middle of the street, idling. Its pitch-black, tinted windows reflected off the moonlight like two big eyes watching me.

The driver didn't roll down the window, didn't honk the horn, or make any sort of gesture to indicate he was there for me. Unease ripped holes in my stomach. I glanced over my shoulder at the locked door, then to the left and right of me.

The car remained in place, and its presence had a direct line to my nerves. I was locked outside the front of this building with no place to run. My driver hadn't shown up or returned my text to let me know when he would be arriving.

Fuck this shit.

I took off, marching down the last few steps before I took to the sidewalk in the direction of my hotel. I was not about to stand there and wait for whoever was inside that vehicle to decide my fate. I was better off taking my chances on the move. That way, I could at least run and hide or run until I found other people.

The BMW's engine revved, and it took everything in me not to glance back. My steps grew faster, and my heart pumped harder, but I kept moving. The sound of the vehicle grew louder with that straining noise a vehicle makes when it's reversing. The sound added tension to my hyped-up senses.

Who the hell was that inside that vehicle, watching me, following me? Was it a crazy person getting their jollies by scaring me? Headlights approached from a distance.

"Lord, please let it be my driver. Please let it be my driver," I prayed out loud.

The Lord was listening because the Tahoe I prayed for pulled to a stop near me. The driver immediately opened his door and climbed out.

A glance over my shoulder showed that the SUV was gone. I was so busy getting away from it that I hadn't seen or even heard when it had taken off.

"Are you okay, Ms. Hendrix? I apologize for arriving a few minutes late. I had a little highway mishap."

"That's okay. I'm fine," I told him, practically diving in the backseat while he held the door open for me. From now on, I wouldn't be going outside and waiting for my ride.

As we drove, this incident brought back the news of Trent getting jacked in their club's parking lot.

Was I reaching or jumping to conclusions to think that the two incidents were tied together? Silence swarmed the cab of the car, but there was a bullhorn inside my head and a voice yelling so loudly I had to close my eyes to process the noise.

"What kind of mishap did you run into?" I asked the driver, trying to put an end to my plaguing thoughts.

"A road-raged driver cut me off. Forced me to pull off and stop on the side of the highway. Then he climbed out of his car and threw up his hands as if asking me what I wanted to do. He tapped his hand against his chest like he wanted to fight before flashing obscene gestures at me. He was acting like I was the one who'd committed the offense. After a long stare-off and me being smart enough to remain inside my vehicle, he climbed back in his car and took off."

"That was rude," I replied. "It sounds about as strange as the incident that just happened to me. A car pulled to a stop in the middle of the road in front of the building where I was standing and waiting for you. I sensed the eyes of whoever was inside watching me. I took off a little before you showed up, unwilling to wait around to see what they wanted."

"I'm so sorry you had to go through that."

"It's okay, but it can't be a coincidence that we both encountered strange occurrences at the same time."

"Are you suggesting the two incidents are tied together?" he asked, glancing up in the rearview mirror.

My fingers raked across the back of my neck, and I absently rubbed the area, not knowing what to believe.

"I don't know, but it is...weird."

A companionable silence fell between us and allowed me to ease back into speculation mode. Had I overreacted? It could have easily been someone on the phone or searching for a building. The person may not have even noticed me standing there.

Why was I feeding myself lies when I'd sensed the tension stirring in the air? Whoever was in that vehicle was watching me. Who was it?

The prickly sense of not knowing was driving me crazy. Why did Trent, just a few nights before my incident, have a car episode that ended with him being jacked for his money? Was I drawing too many conclusions that had nothing to do with each other?

"Do you want me to park and walk you up?" the driver asked, drawing my attention and making me aware that we had arrived and were parked outside the hotel.

"No need," I replied and waited until he exited, walked back, and opened my door.

"Thank you." I took the hand he handed me to help me out of the vehicle.

I had never been so happy to see a hotel in my life. The shower and bed were calling my name so loud I almost answered out loud.

Chapter Fifteen

Trent

My leg bounced, and no matter what I did, hands in pockets, ankle over ankle, it wouldn't stop. Every person who stepped off that escalator and turned toward baggage claim number 12 had my undivided attention. It had only been a week since I'd seen Callie, and the time had dragged on like a month.

Sexy wedged-heeled sneakers, skin-tight, hip-hugging jeans, and a shredded T-shirt cover tank that hung off one shoulder came into view. The woman made articles of clothing look as complicated and unique as collector's items.

Atlas' statement about a designer being as much a model as the models they dressed was true in Callie's case. She was visually stunning, and when you added smart and outgoing, you had a triple threat for the record books.

And she'd agreed to be mine.

My grin couldn't be contained, especially when she spotted me and flashed a brilliant smile right back at me. I couldn't wait. I started out slow and deliberate, and then my pace picked up until I was within reach of her. I didn't wait for her to hug me. I scooped her up and did a little cheesy twirl.

"Mmm," I muttered against her neck, her skin emitting the scent of rose petals.

"I missed the hell out of you," I blurted out against her soft, warm flesh.

"I missed the hell out of you, too," she returned, giggling and returning my hug with a tight one of her own.

Our action drew attention, especially from people at-tempting to get around us to wait for their luggage. We didn't care about the side eyes, snide comments about get-ting a room or even the subtle bumps because we'd fallen into our own little world.

***

It took an eternity for Callie's bag to finally come around that conveyor belt. The longer it took, the more my brain conjured up images of me fucking her while we turned on the belt with the luggage.

When she finally pointed out her bag, I grabbed it and her hand and walked briskly out of the airport.

"Are you in a hurry?" Callie asked, glancing at the speedometer of my car before lifting and settling her eyes on me.

"Oh. Didn't notice how fast we were moving," I re-plied, grinning. I needed to get her back to my place, and time was standing in my way. She'd agreed to come home with me versus returning to her place. The gesture made me feel special.

Now, all I could think about was getting her naked and in my bed.

"I can't lie to you. I can't wait to get you naked. Then, we can talk about the weeks we've had and anything else you'd like to discuss. I'll even draw you a nice hot bubble bath and make you breakfast in bed.

She giggled. "That sounds like an excellent plan."

"I…"

The sudden bright light blinded me and cut off my words.

"Who the hell is this on my ass with their bright lights on?" I mumbled, speeding up a little and hoping the asshole would go on and pass me if they were in a hurry. I was already going fast enough and didn't need to add to the collection of speeding tickets I'd collected throughout the years because my foot was heavy on the gas pedal.

"What are they doing? Why don't they just pass? We're nearing a residential area where there is practically nothing else driving on the road," Callie pointed out, glancing in her side mirror.

The loud roar of the car's engine sounded, forcing an obscene amount of nervous energy into me. What the hell was this guy's problem? I fingered the button to take my window down. Once it was down, I stuck my arm out and waved the driver around me.

Callie rolled down her window and did the same, but the stupid person wouldn't listen. Were they on a mission to irritate the hell out of us?

Bam!

I was thrust forward, my neck snapping fast before the back of my head smashed into the headrest. My car came to a screeching halt from me slamming my foot on the brakes, giving us another quick jerk.

My arm was out and in front of Callie before I even processed what was happening. The asshole had rammed us.

"Are you okay? Are you hurt?" I asked Callie, my face tight with concern and not paying attention to the car that hit us.

"They're leaving. Hey!" Callie yelled at the car that hit us, her eyes following their dwindling taillights. They had taken off, and like the vehicle carrying the vandals who stole my gym bag, this one didn't have a visible license plate either.

I took off, my foot slamming down on the gas pedal.

"You're going to chase them? What if it's a lunatic that's baiting you into a trap to get his jollies. I'm calling the police," Callie said, taking out her phone and dialing while scanning the area to see where we were.

"Yes. I'd like to report a hit-and-run. It happened near the corner of Atlantic Avenue and Canal. My boyfriend and I are following the car, attempting to get a license plate or to at least get them to stop.

"A series of yes's and no's followed Callie's initial statement while the asshole who hit us was getting away. I could barely make out his taillights as he sped recklessly through an otherwise quiet neighborhood like a bat out of hell.

This encounter was the third car-related incident for Callie and me within a week. What was going on? Could this be her ex-boyfriend? Was he attempting to get back at us for a situation that his own wrongdoing had caused? Callie had filed charges, but as she suspected, he wasn't arrested, and we weren't sure he was even questioned.

"You think this could be your ex trying to get back at you for pressing charges on him? If he's targeting me, it means he knows that we're together now."

"I don't think so, but I couldn't imagine him doing something as criminal as drugging me either."

She placed the phone back to her ear, reminding me that she was still on with the police.

"We are no longer following the car. We lost it," she informed the person on the other end. She paused, nodding at what the person was telling her.

"We need to return to the area where your car was hit," she said, glancing in my direction. "The police are on the way."

Thirty-five minutes and all the police did was take a report without so much as mentioning that they would do any other type of work to find out who hit me. Thankfully, the damage to the back of my car was minor scratches and dents that could easily be repaired.

We informed the police about what had happened to Callie with her ex and that we had filed a report for that as well. The taller of the two male officers gave me a what-do-you-want-me-to-do-about-it look, letting me know that Callie and I were on our own.

At this point, we had no idea if we were being targeted by her ex, if one of us genuinely had a stalker, or if we were simply going through a bout of bad luck.

Chapter Sixteen

Callie

"Finally," I breathed, releasing a long exhale. Trent eased off the gas before turning his car into the driveway of a large, two-story brick home. We were in the Scott's Addition area, where I knew the average cost of homes was at least four hundred thousand.

I glanced at him, expecting him to back out of the driveway and say that he was kidding, but he kept going until the garage door began to lift.

"Wow!" I said, straining my eyes to see more details. "You have a beautiful home."

"Thank you," he replied.

Although the stress of the night hadn't entirely died down, it didn't stop me from acknowledging Trent's amazing house.

"I took you to my condo the last time because it was closer," he said before I could ask who's place we'd slept in the night he rescued me from Donni.

"Please don't take this the wrong way, but I didn't think dancers made enough to afford a place like this, let alone two places."

He chuckled.

"The ones who use their money wisely do. I'm under thirty with a degree, a car, a condo, and a house that's paid for. If you ask me, dancing is underrated as a good income source." He lifted a finger to reiterate something. "Sorry, this house will be paid off by the end of the year," he corrected. I could hear the pride in his tone, and he should have been. If he'd used dancing to get this big of a head start in life, then I applauded him.

A bit more of my tension eased when we rolled into his garage, and he cut the car's engine.

He hopped out and marched around to my side to help me out. I slapped my palm into his, smiling up at the big, bright smile he shone down on me.

Warmth and ease were the relaxing vibes that rolled through my body while walking beside him. He keyed the door open before showing me in with a sweeping hand gesture.

"First things first. I'll give you a little tour and make us some much-needed drinks."

My smile spread wide. "Drinks sound great. And I can't wait to see your home."

At the first view of the living room, my eyes darted around the space before I shot a quick glance in his direction.

"You didn't decorate...did you?"

"No," he chuckled. "I did the smart thing and paid someone to do it for me. All I had to do was tell them what colors and styles I liked."

I nodded, seeing the subtle hints of royal blue and splashes of yellow here and there as I passed through the den and entered the kitchen.

"So, is your favorite color blue or yellow?"

"Both," he replied, grinning.

"His kitchen was all granite countertops and stainless steel. He even had a fancy rack with his pots hanging above the island.

"Nice. Do you cook?"

"No," he replied quickly. "Doubt I know how to take one of those pots down." He shrugged with a lighthearted grin on his handsome face.

I laughed.

"You laugh, but I'm one of those who'll somehow manage to burn a pot of water. So, I stay in my lane when it comes to cooking. I save myself the trouble and order my food like the smart man I consider myself to be."

"Yet, you promised to make me breakfast in bed less than an hour ago," I reminded him.

He fake punched the air and laughed, knowing he'd been caught in a lie.

An image of him with a fire extinguisher putting out a burning pot on the stove popped into my head and made me chuckle.

The rest of the tour revealed three bedrooms, three and a half bathrooms, and a small room he had turned into an office.

When the tour ended, he directed me to the big, comfortable couch in the living room.

"Have a seat, and I'll pour our drinks."

His decorator had done an impressive job on his living room, but my eyes were riveted on him and taking an admiring stroll of the back view of him walking to his bar.

"Besides Ransome and Atlas, the decorator, and the realtor who sold me this place, you are the only other person who's been inside my house."

That bit of news got my attention.

"Are you serious?"

He nodded, grinning at my wrinkled forehead and the unblinking stare I pinned on him.

"No housewarming, house parties, no barbecues or anything?"

He kept shaking his head no at my questions while grinning at me.

"I never felt the need for any of that, nor did I want the people I work with in my personal space. Don't get me wrong, I'm friends with a lot of the people I work with and would help them if they are ever in trouble. However, I don't consider them family like I do Atlas and Ransome and, therefore, don't want them in my house."

This man never ceased to amaze me. Like me, he cherished his personal space, and I liked that aspect of him. A year ago, I was given a glimpse into his life, and I loved the parts I saw. Now that I was getting a more in-depth version of him, it made me want and appreciate him that much more.

"I can understand where you're coming from," I finally responded.

Approaching, he handed me the glass of amber liquid that I graciously accepted.

"Mmm," I moaned as the first hit of the liquid burned before it went down smoothly, leaving a warming tingle behind.

"This is good," I said, glancing at the glass in my hand.

"Johnny Walker. Black Label. That'll help ease your mind."

I nodded. It already felt like it was working. Even the ice clinking inside the glass provided some level of ease.

He sat close, staring but not saying anything, which immediately got my attention.

"Are you okay? Truly okay after what just happened," he asked, concern tightening his brows.

I nodded after taking another sip of my drink. "I'm fine. All of these strange incidents are kind of freaking me out, but I'll be okay. I pray we can find out who's behind this if someone *is* targeting us."

"There have been too many coincidences. I've pissed a few women off in my day, but I don't believe any would stalk me at this level and then go after you too? It makes no sense. I'm starting to believe we're being targeted, and I believe it's by your ex."

"I'm starting to think the same," I replied, my face tightening into a frown at the idea of Donni coming after us. All I wanted was to be left alone.

Trent tapped the side of his head, his gaze pinned on mine.

"The police are not going to want to get involved until someone gets hurt or until we do their jobs for them and prove that it's your ex that's stalking us. The craziest part of this whole situation is if it is Donni, he's taking out his frustrations on us for his own wrongdoing."

"I know," I said, slipping into a chorus of my own thoughts. "How do we catch a snake with deep enough pockets to keep himself hidden?" I was talking more to myself than to Trent. How the hell were we going to catch Donni?

The more I thought about it, the more I was convinced it was him. *Why?* He and I had gone our separate ways well over a year ago and had remained cordial. Why would he want to stalk me now, especially when it would call more attention to the wrong he had done?

The light brush of Trent's finger teasing up and down the side of my arm drew my attention. The liquor had me warm and tingly, and Trent's stroke added the desired effect to spark my arousal.

"Trent," I called, my voice low and breathy and not sounding like my own.

"Yes," he said, leaning in and placing a lingering kiss on my neck that sent a strong pang of lust through me and made my pussy throb.

Every caress and squeeze made my heat flare. His lips on my neck, him palming my ass, and his tongue in my mouth. He was covering multiple places at once including my hard nipples through my top with his teeth.

What were we talking about a moment ago?

The man could take me from zero to a hundred in five seconds flat. He eased back with a teasing smirk on his face. We used the little break to pick up our drinks and sip while eye-stalking each other.

"I don't want it to be cool, calm, or even safe. I want you to fuck me. Fuck me like you did when you hardly knew who the hell I was," I heard myself blurt out.

"Shit, Callie. You almost made me spit this drink all over your lap," he said, chuckling before he took my drink and sat it along with his on the coffee table.

Trent leaned in and placed his lips against my ear. "If fucking is what you want, fucking is what you're going to get."

He dropped to the floor, keeping his eyes on mine while he positioned himself in front of my legs on his knees. With his hands atop my knees, he didn't spread them open. He slung them open before his strong hands slid up my legs and gripped my hips. He jerked me down so fast that my lower half collided with his hard abs, the impact making me gasp.

The possessive glint in his eyes met mine. The way his tongue traced his lips while his gaze traveled the span of my body had me fighting a moan. The look alone had my nipples so hard that they hurt rubbing against the inside of my bra.

My shirt flew up my body so fast a ripping sound drew my concern and turned me on at the same time. He reached behind me and unsnapped my bra like a pro before sliding it off and tossing it over the top of the couch with my top.

"Trent," I exhaled sharply, needing to say his name. My panties and pants, once undone, zipped down my legs, my body jerking with each rough tug. He spread my legs with a quickness I didn't expect. Naked from head to toe, I was spread out in front of him now, with my ass hanging off the edge of the couch.

A shiver followed his hand sliding between my breast, down and over my stomach, and lower to the apex of my sex. He stopped, licking his lips before he lifted his heavy gaze to mine.

"I'm about to eat this beautiful pussy, make it purr for me, and treat it with some respect. Then, I'm going to fuck you so hard, and with so much disrespect, it will be me you're calling the police on."

Damn! That sounded like a promise I prayed he wouldn't break.

"Oh, fuck!" I yelled when his mouth melted into my pussy. He sucked my clit like it was a piece of caramel melting on the tip of his tongue.

I twirled my hips, chasing his mouth and praising his magnificent tongue.

"Baby," I grunted the cry, the word buzzing in my throat before it lit the air. "Feels so good." I vaguely heard myself say. My stomach muscles flexed while my hips worked in time with them to catch every last juicy drop of the mouth and tongue action he lavished on me.

"You taste like my sweetest fucking fantasy. This pussy has always had my name on it. You just didn't know it."

He licked me with a firmer intensity and teased my clit with quick twirls.

"And I'm going to make sure it will always be mine."

"Shit," I moaned. Pleasure raced through me so hard that I swore I was possessed.

"Tell me it's mine. That it will always be mine."

My pussy quivered at the sound of his voice, speaking for me. The ache of the sweet devastation looming over me threatened to reach down and take me out.

My heart pumped. My legs shook. My lady parts vibrated. I couldn't catch a breath to save my life, but the sensations rolling through me made me forget about all I was unable to do at that moment.

"Trent. Oh. Trent. You know it's yours!" I yelled before he did more tongue acrobatics that sliced across my clit and teased my walls repeatedly until I saw stars.

"T...t..." I couldn't spit out one syllable. I didn't know where the hell I was. Wherever it was, only an unlimited number of the most decadent sensations known to humanity lived here, and they were all traveling through me.

I had no idea how much time had passed when reality decided to check back in. I could hardly lift my head. My legs were splayed wide open, and my brown, blush-kissed skin glistened with a light sheen of sweat.

Trent had that look on his face. A look that said I better prepare myself because he wasn't done.

"Aww!" I yelled when he flipped my ass. I hadn't even seen him move.

My stomach smashed into the edge of the couch when he lifted me, positioning my ass up before he delivered a hard slap that made me scream his name.

"Trent!"

I didn't know if I was screaming in protest or aiming to get him to ease up. Either way, I would have to take whatever was coming. He ran his hand across my stinging behind and dragged it down until his finger slid between the crack of my ass. His fingertip stopped right on my star, rubbing it lightly. His other hand was around my side, his fingers dancing against my clit, making me slick all over again.

"Damn, you're dripping wet, baby. You want this dick, don't you? Tell me you want it."

I glanced back across my shoulder, riding his finger, loving the sensation he was driving into multiple areas.

"I want the dick," I said, dropping my gaze in time to see him grip his thick shaft and squeeze. A pearl of pre-cum dripped down the head, the sight widening my eyes and sending a thrilling ache through me that had wet heat leaking down my inner thighs.

My waist was gripped, my ass was aligned, and...

"Oh! Shit!" I yelled out in a long scream the neighbors probably heard at the hard pounding thrust that sent Trent deep inside me. Pain rode the wave of pleasure and gave me a full-body tremor.

"You will take every inch of this dick."

It was a command.

"Take," he backed out and pushed back in, even harder.

"This," he continued, backing out again and thrusting into me with so much force, the damn couch grunted against our movement.

"Dick," he finished, pounding hard enough to knock my damn top knot loose, sending my hair spilling all over my head.

There wasn't shit I could do but take the hard pounding that rocked my whole body. I was at his mercy, and he currently wasn't in the mood to be merciful. Each thrust hit so deeply the head licked my cervix, and I believed it was knocking the lining off my damn walls.

"Fuck!" I shouted. "Why?" I asked.

Why was this so fucking good? Shouldn't I be in pain? Shouldn't I be begging him to take it easy on me?

"Deep. So fucking deep. Tell me you like it deep, Callie. Tell me you like me fucking you hard and rough."

"I like..." I struggled to focus. " I li...lik... Tren..." I couldn't think. My vocal cords were only working when they wanted to.

Stone cold mad. This man drove me past that point. All that he was saying about my pussy belonging to him was true. Hell, if it wasn't true before, he was making it so now.

"Trent," I heaved out his name. "Trent," I said, groaning loud and harshly.

"I know, baby. Your pussy is telling my dick all it needs to know, " he replied.

I didn't teeter or tip over or even fall. My ass dived clean off the cliff of pleasure and rode the euphoric thrill all the way down to a magnificent orgasmic world of tranquil bliss.

My mouth dropped open, and I didn't know if sound was coming out or not because my world was shattered in the most brilliant way possible.

"Fuck, Callie. Fuck!" Trent's voice was distant, and his pounding was relentless until he came to a quick stop. His body quivered, and his curse words were a jumble of sounds that expressed his heightened state of pleasure.

They say to be careful what you wish for, but in this case, Trent made sure my damn wish had come true.

Chapter Seventeen

Callie

"Say what now?" Dayton asked, cupping her ear for dramatic effect after my announcement.

"You've been sneaking and freaking around with a stripper too? Dayem!" she exclaimed, lips hanging open and eyes zeroed in on me.

She blew out a long breath like she'd just received life-changing news, and her teasing gaze bounced back and forth between Charlene and me.

"That super-freak shit they do on stage must follow them home," she muttered under her breath. "They got my girls. They got my damn girls," she mumbled, low but audible enough for us to hear. She was doing too much.

Charlene and I pursed our lips and gave Dayton the eye for being melodramatic.

"All she just revealed to us about her and Trent possibly being stalked by her ex, and that's all you take from the story?" Charlene asked Dayton the question while leveling her with a chastising stare.

Dayton met her stiff gaze with one of her own.

"Let me process this situation the way I want to, please. This one—" Dayton turned in my direction and looked me up and down with her nose scrunched up like I stunk.

"This one has been sneaking around us with a stripper for over a year and is just now telling us. Oh, and let's not forget, hanging out with her dumb ass ex, who I told her gave off psycho vibes when she was dating him. The motherfucker growled at me that time at the club for calling him out for staring at our girl like she was a fucking raw steak and he the ravenous wolf."

Charlene lifted a brow, and I knew her well enough that the little hitch in her brow meant she found truth in what Dayton was saying. Was I the only one who hadn't seen the crazy they had pointed out in Donni?

He'd been over the top about spending time with me, often butting heads with my friends when they planned our girl time. I'd taken the gesture as a compliment, glad my man wanted to spend time with me. I'd had to find out the hard way that his motives weren't admirable.

"I can't believe he drugged you. What if Trent hadn't been there?" Charlene asked, stress lines visible on her forehead.

Absently, I shook my head. "I don't know what would have happened. I assumed Donni understood that we were friends. We even talked on the phone every once in a while, and he never gave the impression that he wanted anything other than a friendship."

"I hate to say this," Dayton said.

"No, you don't," Charlene interjected, cutting her eyes at Dayton, who rarely *hated* to say anything. She was the most outspoken of the three of us. She ignored Charlene and proceeded with her monologue.

"Like I said, I *hate* to say this, but your biggest mistake was keeping in contact with him. Every time you talked to him, he saw it as a chance. It didn't matter if you two were talking about the weather; the conversation counted as a chance at getting you back. That's the way some men are wired. Donni was waiting for an opportunity to wiggle his way back into your life, and when he finally found one, he went for it."

I couldn't deny that Dayton was speaking the truth regarding Donni's intentions.

"I'm guessing that he didn't want to take a chance of not getting to where he wanted things to go with you sexually, so he decided to drug you. And that shit is serious. It speaks for his mental stability. He could have taken you someplace and raped you. And if he's a real sicko like I believe he is, he could have locked you up in a basement prison or some shit crazy people like him do."

The image Dayton's words conjured made me shiver. I had dodged a bullet when I decided to leave him. Trent had helped me dodge another bullet from my failure to truly see Donni for the creep he was.

"I didn't let my thoughts go that far," I finally replied to Dayton.

Charlene eyeballed Dayton before shaking her head at her.

"Sometimes, I wonder about you. Haven't you learned to just keep some stuff to yourself? I didn't believe Donni would hurt Callie either. The man has built an online image that screams well-put-together and approachable. His family's sketchy past adds just enough danger to his background to heighten people's intrigue about him," Charlene pointed out, always the voice of reason.

"Those are the ones you have to watch the most," Dayton stated. "The ones who look perfect on the outside. The ones with the factory-built personalities." She didn't miss a beat. "Since we're talking about men. How well do you know Trent? The man literally set the stage on fire with his fireman routine. Does he have a pole in his house? Has he given you any one-on-one dances?"

"Really, Dayton? Really? That's where you're choosing to take this conversation?" Charlene questioned, fighting not to laugh. "Like I said before, I wonder about what goes on in that head of yours."

Dayton shrugged, unfazed by Charlene's questions, comments, and sharp side-eye.

"I'm glad he was there to save you from that Cosby copycat, but why was Trent clocking you in the first place? You might be playing hot potato with two stalkers," she pointed out.

"Lord, why? Why do I love this crazy-ass woman who will let anything slide out of her mouth?" Charlene asked, staring up at the ceiling before she joined me in cutting our eyes at Dayton.

"Trent is nothing like Donni," I defended. "He treats me like I matter. He listens to me when I speak, responds, and provides insight. He's different from any of the men I've dated. I would never lump him in the category with the likes of Donni."

Charlene placed a calming hand atop mine while Dayton stroked up and down my back since I'd gotten surprisingly emotional talking about Trent. Dayton had a smart mouth on her, but she cared about my feelings and what I was going through, whether she said so or not.

"You care about Trent, don't you?" Charlene asked, her hand stroking mine in a motherly fashion.

"I do. I care about him a lot. He's nothing like the role he plays on that stage. He's so much more and has so much more to offer. I recognized it a year ago and also recently when we decided to give our relationship a chance."

"Oh," Dayton said, lifting a brow. "That explains some things."

"It does?" Charlene and I questioned simultaneously, our faces pinched in curiosity.

She nodded like a scholarly professor about to school her students. Dayton was always the first to offer up relationship advice but avoided the same advice she dished out like the plague, just as she avoided relationships.

"I believe Donni noticed you with Trent, your vibe with him, and I'd bet my left tit that Donni's reaction was all about jealousy. Men are fucking fragile babies when they see something they want, like a woman they want with another man. They get especially cray-cray when they see another man giving her things like love, affection, financial support, or whatever they couldn't or don't know how to give her themselves."

My face squinted, my thoughts scattered now. "Donni saw me briefly talking to Trent, but I don't believe he saw us together long enough to determine that we may have had feelings for one another. I don't think he noticed that me and Trent were more than friends until after he drugged me."

Dayton shook her head, her lips pursing with doubt. "If you were all at the same party, trust me, that stalker had eyes on you—you just didn't know it. The crazy thing is if he was willing to go so far as to drug you, does it mean he's been stalking you?"

Charlene glanced up, the glint in her eyes unreadable. "You've never dated anyone after Donni, other than the weekend you spent with Trent a year ago. Right?"

Reluctantly, I nodded at her. After that weekend with Trent, I had no desire to date, so I poured all of my time into work.

Charlene reclaimed my attention when she continued. "It meant that Donni didn't have a reason to get jealous of anyone until he saw you with Trent."

My brain overflowed with the different aspects of dissecting my situation. But there was one question that continued to nag me that I would have liked answered.

"How do I prove now that it might be Donni stalking Trent and me? What if it isn't him?"

Dayton scooted to the edge of her seat, her expression the most serious of the night.

"You were right the first time. How do we prove the sick asshole is stalking you? Even if it isn't him, we can't ignore that he committed a crime when he drugged you."

I swallowed the rush of emotions that her statements and Charlene's co-signing headshake spurred. She was right. They were right. Either way, I'd have to deal with Donni.

"We pulled off a smooth breaking and entering plot to get Carter's conniving ass off Charlene's back. But we're not doing the same thing for you because I can't see myself scaling a high rise attempting to break into a penthouse. What floor is the asshole on again?" Dayton asked.

"The twenty-ninth floor," I answered.

"Nope, we can't break into his place," she mumbled, her eyes fixed straight ahead as she concentrated on whatever was rolling through her head.

"You can play the damsel in distress and see if you can get him to confess," Charlene suggested. Dayton immediately shook her head at the suggestion.

"Even if she got him to confess to everything, I'm sure he has an elite attorney on retainer that can get him off without any jail time. We want him to go to jail, just like Carter's ass is in jail now," she continued.

Charlene's ex had blackmailed her to stay with him all while he'd gotten a seventeen-year-old girl pregnant. Charlene had hired a private investigator to dig up dirt on her ex, and Dayton and I had helped her break into the apartment her ex rented for the girl for more information. The detective's information, along with all the information Charlene had uncovered on her own, was enough to land her ex in jail.

Dayton drummed her fingers on the couch seat next to her leg, her brain working overtime for a way to catch Donni slipping. "If he was drugging you, he's probably done that foul shit before. If we could find other women he's done it to who would be willing to talk, it could be a start. There could also be other charges out against him for the same thing. If he has a pattern of drugging women, then it could spark something bigger."

We stared at each other long and hard, our eyes and facial expressions holding a silent conversation.

"Where do we even start?" Charlene asked. "He's got money. Social media influence. His parents have ties to the streets."

Donni had some elements in his life that would make it difficult to catch or prove his wrongdoing, but he wasn't untouchable. Everyone had weaknesses.

Dayton's mischievous smile made me shake my head. Did I even want to know what was rummaging around in her brain?

"I have an idea," Dayton said, eyeing Charlene and me, who glanced at each other before setting our gazes back on our friend.

She was about to take a page from *The Book of Dayton* and lead us into temptation before attempting to deliver us from whatever evil we stirred. After all was said and done, I just prayed we didn't end up in jail

Chapter Eighteen

Trent

"Who the fuck does this guy think he is?" Ransome asked. It was the third question in a row that I hadn't answered because I couldn't.

"How could someone like Callie fall for an egotistical asshole like that?" Atlas tacked on a statement disguised as a question.

Callie's ex, Donni, had been under our watchful eyes for the past three days. We had become stalkers, following the man's car and trailing him to his friends, parties, events, his penthouse, and now his house out in the sticks.

We hadn't found anything we could use against him other than his asshole ways. He was rude to everyone, didn't leave good tips at restaurants, eye-fucked every woman he found attractive, and talked shit to the ones who weren't interested in him.

He deserved nothing less than a good ass-beating or jail time for what he did to Callie and possibly other women. Callie meant too much to me to just wait while the authorities did nothing. I refused to sit idly by while he ran around free and clear to plan his next date-rape fantasy. Ransome and Atlas agreed to help me without question.

"Hand me those binoculars," I told Ransome, who'd been hugging them to be nosey.

"Is he…?" Atlas started but stopped talking so he could focus on seeing better, I supposed. Face squinted, and eyes peeled and straining, he struggled to see through the smaller binoculars. We had a bird's eye view of

Donni's second-floor bedroom from the open balcony doors and wall of glass with open drapes.

"Is he putting drugs in his fucking belt buckle?"

"Let me see. Let me see," Ransome whisper-yelled, attempting to take the binoculars from Atlas when he couldn't pull mine from my tight grip.

"The son-of-a-bitch is about to go someplace and drug another unsuspecting woman so he can do some foul shit to her later," I muttered through clenched teeth.

I tracked his movements, watching the asshole walk out of his bedroom. A moment later, he reappeared in his living room, where the view was blurred due to the thin, closed drapes.

A few minutes later, he walked out of his house to a car waiting in his driveway. His driver didn't even get a hello when he opened the back door for the prick.

They took off, but we waited, parked off the tree-lined street outside his gated property. Atlas pulled off when they were far enough ahead of us not to suspect being followed.

I rode shotgun while Ransome sat in the back behind me. Atlas had taken one for the team. He'd screwed a lead detective whose pillow talk resulted in the inside scoop on Donni, including his address as well as verbal confirmation that he had two other cases pending against him. Unsurprisingly, one of the cases involved a woman who had put a restraining order on him for drugging and stalking her.

Now, at a little after eleven p.m., we were following his car into the parking lot of Club Sensation and watching his driver drop him at the VIP entrance. I didn't doubt that Donni had every intention of using those drugs to incapacitate an unsuspecting woman.

Knowing this brought to light a pressing dilemma. How far did we let Donni take this situation to get the proof we needed to send his ass to jail?

We had every intention of stopping him from the final disrespectful act. However, the idea of standing by and letting him drug a woman didn't sit well with me. The idea of sitting by and allowing him to take her out of the club was even more disturbing. But how else were we supposed to get physical proof of his crimes?

***

Callie

"Me, Charlene, and Dayton are hanging out tonight," I told Trent, holding the phone tight against my ear, since ears were listening in on my side of the conversation. It wasn't a total lie I'd told him. I just didn't mention to him me and my friends intentions for the night.

"Are you still going to have your male bonding time with Ransome and Atlas?" I asked, changing the subject.

"Yes," Trent replied quickly. I could hear loud music in the background. He must have been at Club Chaos picking up the guys because tonight wasn't one of his dance nights. I wanted to be nosey, but didn't want to keep him on the phone any longer than necessary.

"You guys have fun. I'll see you tomorrow."

"I can't wait," Trent growled. "Have a wonderful night, but not too much fun that you're not at full strength for me tomorrow."

I chuckled. "Okay. Good night. Miss you," I sang the last parting note into the phone.

Two sets of beautifully made-up eyes were set on me, the sight causing a wide smile to crease my face. Dayton placed a finger in the hollow of her open mouth and faked puking. Charlene, on the other hand, looked like a proud mamma hen.

"You done?" Dayton asked.

"You really like him, don't you?" Charlene followed up. She'd asked me the question before, but I believe she needed to be reassured that I was sure about pursuing a serious relationship with Trent.

"Yes, I'm done," I answered Dayton first, aiming a stiff warning finger at her. "I can't wait until you find your person. I'm going to let you have every bit of attitude I can muster up and tease you every chance I get."

I lifted a hand before she could hit me with a slick remark and turned my gaze on Charlene.

"Yes, I do like him."

The heavy sigh Dayton released behind us broke into mine and Charlene's corny smiling and hand-holding episode. There was no doubt we resembled two ladies in church preparing for the sermon of our lives.

"Are you two ready to do this?" Dayton asked. She meant ready to embrace the trouble we were likely about to stir up in this club. I'd prayed consistently for the past few days that this plan we'd hatched would work.

"Yes," we finally answered.

***

Thank goodness I'd had a few drinks before we left Dayton's place. The liquid courage worked wonders on my confidence by keeping the nervousness I should have felt at bay.

"I see him," Charlene said, patting my forearm to get my attention.

"You're up, Dayton," I said. She stood, ready, her face awash with determination. She was eager to get things rolling, the only one of us not filled with tension and nervous energy.

I reached out and caught Dayton's arm, stopping her from storming off.

"You don't have to do this. We can always go straight to plan B."

She patted my arm, pity for me reflected in her gaze.

"Let's stick to the plan. We need to take that pussy-stealing bastard down."

She was right, but Charlene couldn't fight the grimace of concern she flashed as Dayton walked her crazy butt away.

We stared until Dayton mingled into the crowd. Charlene and I used the same crowd to inch our way closer to Dayton's location to keep her in our sights.

She didn't spring right into action. She danced with a guy for a few minutes, no doubt scoping out the scene before she made her way to the bar. She leaned across the bar, right next to where Donni sat on a stool, staring at the dance floor with a drink in his hand.

He glanced at Dayton briefly, his gaze trailing down her body and back up, and a palpable lust I could almost feel emanated from his disgusting face. The man was a filthy pig.

Once upon a time, I believed I loved him and swore that he was a good guy. Now I'm sorry it took me this long to acknowledge that he was a great actor and that I was nothing more than a fool under his influence. Was it because of his status? His fake charm?

When Donni's gaze finally made it up to the side of Dayton's face, recognition caused him to ease his head back before his eyes went wide. He tapped the side of her arm. The lust in his eyes was still there, appearing to have grown stronger now that he recognized her.

Dayton ignored him while she worked on gaining the bartender's attention, so Donni sent another tap against her arm, this time drawing her attention.

Charlene and I were like two low-budget detectives, keeping tabs on the situation from afar. With the cheap listening devices we bought from the Project Security store, we were running our own little sting operation. I prayed we didn't end up the ones getting stung.

"You're Callie's friend," I barely heard him say. He sounded scratchy and distorted through the device. His words were being broken apart by the crowd and music, but we were close enough to read his lips.

"Dayton," she replied, leaning further across the bar to flirt with the bartender who had shown up and was clearly interested in her.

Donni's eyes were all over Dayton's body. He didn't hide the fact that he was checking her out. The sight of him checking her out without an ounce of guilt made disgust churn in my gut.

"How's Callie?" he asked her, ignoring the flirt-session she had going on with the bartender.

She flashed the bartender a friendly smile before turning to Donni. The smile she'd been flashing a second ago disappeared. The sadness on her face now was real enough that I would have become concerned if we hadn't already practiced the lines she would feed him.

She shrugged, and her chin dropped to her chest while she glanced up at him through her lashes, her eyes sparking with sadness. The prolonged silence she projected made him turn further toward her on his bar stool.

"What do you mean you don't know how Callie is?" he asked her. She shrugged again, her posture hunched in defeat.

"I know that you and I haven't gotten along well in the past, but I'm worried about her more now than ever before," Dayton said, eyeing him with a pleading expression like she was crying out for his help.

He asked her something else, but I couldn't hear it because of the noise from the crowd. Was that concern on his face? Who was I kidding? It was a practiced face he'd perfected, his attempt to convince Dayton that he cared.

"She's going out with this stripper," Dayton said, glancing down and picking at the napkin the bartender had placed before her.

I hated to use Trent's job title as a part of our scheme, but if there was one thing Donni assumed, it was that he was better than everybody else. He especially hated Trent after Trent had confronted him and rescued me from his grimy grips.

"She..." Dayton struggled with getting her words out, swallowing hard and blinking her eyes like she was fighting tears. The bartender sat her drink in front of her, and Donni placed his hand atop hers when she reached out to hand the bartender a few bills.

The bartender nodded in Donni's direction after picking up the bills he'd thrown down.

Donni kept his hand atop Dayton's, staring at their connection like he was possessed by it. He fingered her arm, allowing his creep mentality to show before glancing up at her and nodding. He waited expectantly for her to complete the statement. She placed a hand over her chest, closed her eyes, and breathed herself back together.

I saw a small portion of Dayton's face at this angle, not enough to decipher her reactions. But I pictured her fighting hard not to cringe at Donni's touch.

"That guy is no good for Callie. He's convinced her that everyone else is against her, or bad for her. He is alienating her from everyone who cares about her."

Donni eyed Dayton with a palpable curiosity after that statement. Dayton pointed a finger at Donni while allowing her body to shake with heavy emotion.

"I was wrong about you. Callie was so much better off with you in her life."

His small smile gradually spread into a wide grin. Dayton was spot on telling him that I had a problem. His smile spoke volumes about how he truly felt about my issues. His ego was in love with the idea of me being unhappy without him, that I needed him.

"He even convinced Callie that you drugged her. Can you believe that shit? And he's so good at his lies that she believed him?" Dayton continued, laying it on thick.

She'd hit a home run with Donni now. He was eating up her twisted retelling of my troubles like it was candy.

"Where is she?" he questioned. He turned slightly in his seat, glancing around. He appeared to look directly at me, but his eyes kept scanning the club.

"Is she here?"

Dayton nodded. "She's here, searching for...*him*. He's supposed to be here tonight."

"Will you take me to her? I care about Callie and won't let some two-bit stripper mess up her life," he muttered, downing his drink and slamming the glass on the counter. He threw a few bills beside the glass and stood.

Dayton picked up her drink, and even from a distance, I saw her trying to keep from smiling. Charlene and

I tore through the crowd, returning to our reserved table in a quiet area. We had roles to play.

Chapter Nineteen

Trent

"There goes that motherfucker again. And he's with Callie's friend," Atlas pointed out.

My head jerked around so fast that I was surprised it didn't spin off my damn shoulders.

"You've gotta be kidding me. Callie's friend is an asshole for messing with her ex, but we can't let him drug her. She has no idea the kind of snake that sick fuck is," I gritted out, biting deep into my lip.

"I'll run interference," Atlas volunteered and marched off before we could stop him.

Fuck!

Shit was about to hit the fan if we didn't control this chaos. The solid plan we assumed was well thought out went off the rails the moment we stepped into this club.

"We better stay close to him," I told Ransome, aiming a finger over my shoulder at Atlas. "You know as well as I do that Atlas may look harmless and friendly but will be the first one to throw a punch if shit pops off."

"You're right. Let's go," Ransome mouthed, his forehead creased tightly with concern.

It didn't take but a hot minute for us to spot Atlas approaching Dayton and Donni.

"Not too close," I called to Ransome, catching his arm to stop him before Donni spotted us.

"Hey, don't I know you?" Atlas walked up to Dayton and asked. Ransome and I were close enough to hear them.

Atlas ignored Donni and blocked Dayton's path to prevent her from going any further with the drug pusher.

The frown on her face would have made a lesser man shrink into the floor, but Atlas smiled at her like they were already acquainted.

"Excuse me," Donni glanced across Dayton's shoulder before he took a possessive step closer and lifted a questioning palm. "Don't you see me standing here?"

Atlas didn't acknowledge that the asshole had even spoken. Instead, he kept his gaze pinned on Dayton, his action a smooth brush-off, and no doubt an insult to Donni's overinflated ego.

What was Dayton doing with her face and eyes? Her gaze kept darting to the left with quick flicks in Donni's direction. At his angle, Donni couldn't see her face. Was it a coded gesture she was attempting to make, or was I reading her actions all wrong?

Atlas squinted at her, struggling to discern the subtle movements she proceeded to make. Donni's raging stare was potent enough to cause physical damage for continuing to be ignored by Atlas.

When Donni grew tired of the blatant disrespect, he reached past Dayton and waved a hand in front of Atlas' face.

"Hey, dumb ass, don't you see me standing here. She's with me, doesn't know you, and is clearly not interested. Now, beat it."

From where I was standing, Dayton was more engaged with Atlas than she was with Donni, and it was driving his flaring anger enough for him to speak for her.

He waved a dismissive hand at Atlas, who glanced up and met his tight-set face, but didn't offer a comment. He acted as if Donni was no more than an annoying gnat he needed to swat away.

Donni glanced around the club like he was trying to determine if this was actually happening.

Atlas took Dayton's hand, holding it longer than was appropriate for a woman he didn't know. She didn't pull away from the prolonged caress, so Atlas proceeded to lift her hand to his lips, kissing the back while keeping admiring eyes on her.

The move made Dayton lift a dramatic eyebrow, her gaze deadlocked on Atlas' lips on the back of her hand. It was a dramatic movie seen in the making; the jealous lover hovering at his woman's back while another man swoops in and snatches her attention. Atlas was way off-script.

Donni seethed while observing the scene play out so closely in front of him. Other eyes were on the display, some people pointing, particularly at Donni, and whispering to each other.

Chest rising and falling hard and fast, Donni struggled to contain his building rage at being publicly disrespected.

"I don't see a ring on her finger, and I'm talking to *her*, not you," Atlas finally responded to Donni's long-forgotten question. When he lifted his daring gaze to finally meet Donni's hot one, the tension in the room grew thick enough to suffocate innocent bystanders.

Atlas' face creased into a knot of pure rage while he stared at his fuming adversary. When he made a move to step closer to Donni, Dayton pressed a firm hand against Atlas' chest to keep him in place.

"It's not that serious," Dayton muttered to Atlas and did something funny with her eyes again. Body coiled with roaring tension, Atlas' gaze remained pinned on

Donni. Locked in a heated standoff, neither man made a move to back away from the other.

When Atlas glanced up and spotted Ransome and me approaching them from the sidelines, he shook his head, warning us to stay away.

He bent, leaning in before whispering something in Dayton's ear. The action earned him a hard chest shove from Donni and had me and Ransome running to stop them from causing a bigger scene.

"Is everything alright here?" I asked, walking up and standing beside Atlas, whose fists were balled up at his sides, his breathing erratic, his eyes twitching with anger.

Donni aimed a stiff, angry finger at Atlas.

"Your disrespectful-ass friend doesn't know how to take a hint. She doesn't want him," Donni said, using his head as a pointer between Dayton and Atlas.

Donni's forehead creased with tension, and his gaze became fixed with a sense of knowing when it landed on me.

"You," he gritted out, his anger an out-of-control fire.

"All my friend here is trying to do is protect this woman from a predator like you," I muttered through clenched teeth, fighting to contain my own flaring rage.

"Trent," a delicate voice called, breaking through the thick cloud of tension and noise surrounding us. Callie marched closer to me, her focus on the dramatic scene in progress.

A river of pride washed over me when she parked herself right next to me. Donni's gaze bounced back and forth between us. The veins in his neck and forehead protruded, and his eyes became a flaming pool of fury.

"Callie. You don't have to lower your standards and settle for this loser. Come back to me, baby, and we can talk about things." He tempered his voice in an attempt to sway Callie's decision.

He reached for her hand, but she ignored it, leaving him hanging.

"We can work things out," he continued like he wasn't surrounded by a group of wolves waiting to pounce on him.

"Who the fuck are you calling a loser, you fucking sex-stealing freak," I spat, jumping in Donni's face only to have Ransome and Atlas pull me back.

Donni allowed a condescending grin to fill his face. He hadn't even flinched at my outburst.

He turned his gaze away from me and aimed his manipulative eyes at Callie, even as I did my best to break Atlas and Ransome's hold on me.

"Like I was saying, baby…" His hand brushed Callie's shoulder, stroking it lightly in an attempt to lure her into his net.

"Leave that fucking broke-ass joke alone and come back to me."

My face creased into a tight knot when I gathered that Donni was either the most arrogant man on the planet or crazy. I charged at him and would have punched him square in the jaw if Ransome and Atlas hadn't stopped me.

Donni lifted his hand and made a circling motion. From the crowd, corners of the room, and behind pillars stepped men—his men. There were at least five or six who approached. Some stood behind him, and some remained in the distance, sizing our group up.

I didn't care about his goon squad. I was too busy struggling to get at him. With a smug smirk on his face, he took a step closer to me.

"Take a look around before you leap, frog. Wouldn't want you to end up…well, you know?"

"You think I care about how many men you've hired to fight for you? I'll still mop this floor with your ass," I yelled. With my neck veins taut and my muscles pulled tight enough to snap, I was ready to rip that smug grin off his face.

"I wish you would lay a hand on me. I'll fuck up your world so bad, you'll beg rock-bottom to take you back," he had the nerve to spit at me before his heated expression turned into a condescending grin.

He reached down and placed a hand on Callie's arm again, and she jerked away.

"Don't you touch her, you fucking lunatic!"

Callie turned to me, placing a delicate hand against my chest. Her connection sent a calming vibe into me that dissolved a portion of my rage. I calmed enough for Ransome and Atlas to let go of my arms.

With her eyes locked with mine, Callie said, "Let's go, baby," and waited for me to acknowledge her.

I nodded, and the tight grips of anger holding me in place loosened but didn't let go of me.

"Callie, don't be a fucking fool. You're too good for him. He can't elevate you. He's only going to use you to make a come-up. He's nothing but poor, white, drug-addicted trash."

Each word was an invisible punch to my gut. I'd had enough of the privileged asshole. I scooted Callie to the side and took an angry step forward.

"You motherfucker!" I gritted out.

I didn't know I'd cocked my fist back until I released it and let it sail through the air like a tossed grenade. Right before my knuckles connected with Donni's face, a hard punch caught me in the temple, and another connected with my opposite jaw, staggering me.

Callie and her friends had thankfully been pushed further away by Atlas and Ransome before all hell broke loose. My gaze zoomed in on Donni, who had cowardly stepped back while his men advanced us.

Her friends struggled to restrain Callie, who stood feet away, yelling for us to stop.

"Trent, he's not worth it. Stop it. Please!"

I vaguely heard Callie's calls, but the floodgates had been cracked open too wide to contain the swirling chaos. As soon as Atlas and Ransome stepped away from the ladies, Donni's men charged us.

Fists connected with bodies. Curse words flew around like musical notes. Bodies tussled, a few pulling off what I believed were wrestling moves while others threw wild punches. This was all going down while Donni stood in the background, laughing at us.

His team of fighters came at us relentlessly, aiming to do physical harm. Although none of us had any professional training, we held our own against the six who jumped us and fought to gain the upper hand.

By the time the bouncers separated us, three big burly men in all black, I couldn't say who had won the fight. All I knew was that I had gone toe-to-toe with an eighteen-wheeler. Ripped shirt, aching teeth, and spitting blood between sore lips—I was a mess. Ransome and Atlas looked like they had tumbled down the side of a mountain.

"Get the fuck out of my club and don't ever return!" the tall Asian man, I presume was the owner, yelled at us, his stiff finger aimed in the direction of the nearest exit.

Donni and his men stood behind the man, snickering like this was their normal routine. Donni's probing eyes zoomed in on Callie, who was back at my side, wiping blood from my lips.

If I could have talked without my teeth rattling, I would have told that motherfucker to go eat shit, find a fast-moving train, and step out in front of it. However, I believed that seeing Callie taking care of me hurt him far worse than any of my verbal insults.

Our plan had gone to hell and burned to ashes in one of its fiery pits. However, there was another pressing issue to consider. Why the hell were Callie and her friends here when they were supposed to be at home drinking and talking shit about us? Why the hell was her friend Dayton hanging around with her ex in the first place?

Donni was an asshole, but he was a powerful one who could ruin our lives with the snap of his grimy fingers. Looking at Callie, I prayed that she and her friends weren't up to what I thought they were up to in this club tonight.

Chapter Twenty

Trent

I hated to separate from Callie, but they insisted on meeting us at my place. The women thought they were slick, claiming to need to pick up Callie's car from Dayton's. But, I was betting that they wanted to have a girl-power meeting so they could get their story straight, regroup, and come up with another plan.

Back in the club parking lot, Atlas had to stop Ransome from tossing Charlene across his shoulder and disappearing with her to keep her away from further trouble. She was already receiving hostile glances and remarks from the law enforcement community after her ex was thrown into jail. Now, this shit.

I may never have had a long-time girlfriend, but I had enough good sense not to press a woman too hard. I would have to tiptoe my way around this subject and how best to handle it around Callie and her friends. I continued working it out in my head. How was I going to convince Callie to let me handle her ex?

Although Ransome never said it, he was upset that Charlene never told him that her ex was blackmailing her until after she had found a way to send him to jail. I was grateful she hadn't told him because as crazy as Ransome was over Charlene, I'm sure he'd be the one in jail right now.

Callie knew a lot about me, but I hadn't revealed the specifics of the hard life my mother and I had lived, including a year on the mean streets of California.

We'd had to do some questionable activities or perish under the crushing weight of the unforgiving streets. If shit went sideways as it had tonight, I wanted to be the one to take whatever trouble came with it.

Ransome parked, and I hopped out of his car like the front seat was on fire. I was already texting Callie by the time Atlas and Ransome marched up my driveway and entered the front door. Just as the women were probably strategizing, we had to devise another plan, too.

"Fuck!" I yelled out at the ceiling.

"We fucked that up," Atlas pointed out the obvious, pressing his fingers against a bruise on his cheek. Ransome sat on my couch with his forehead in his palm, his leg bouncing up and down. I believe he was stressing about Charlene being a part of more drama.

I didn't blame him. I was just getting a better understanding of the different levels of stress you could experience over a woman, now that I had someone special of my own.

"The ladies were at that club for the same reason we were. Dayton kept trying to send me hand and eye signals before shit went downhill," Atlas pointed out.

"I gathered that much," I replied dryly.

"How do we get someone who's set himself up to be untouchable. His intentions were to drug someone tonight, and we could have caught him in the act. Now, he's going to be on our asses like white on rice, so catching him doing his dirt will be next to impossible," I said, spitting out the words before I released a loud huff of frustration.

The sound of a car driving up and the flash of headlights in the window drew our attention. Car doors slammed, and clicking heels followed, prompting me to the door. I sprang the door open before Dayton could ring the doorbell. A step back and sweeping hand gesture prompted them to enter.

"Ladies," I greeted. As serious as the situation was, I couldn't stifle the smile that surfaced at the site of Callie. When she reached up and threw her arms around my neck, I automatically folded her into my tight embrace.

"Are you okay?" My question was whispered into her hair before I placed a delicate kiss on her cheek. A loud clap broke up our little reunion.

"Can all the couples in the room save all this hugging and snuggling for later? We have serious business to discuss, like what the hell you ladies called yourselves doing tonight?" Atlas asked.

Dayton leveled him with a serious side-eye while Ransome and Charlene sat on the loveseat, and Callie and I sat next to Dayton on the couch. Atlas stood with his hands behind his back, pacing like he was a professor.

"We were attempting to get that low-down nasty dog to trip himself up so we could send his ass to jail," Dayton replied.

Atlas appeared to breathe a sigh of relief. Dayton noticed, one brow lifted over her curious gaze that was aimed at him.

"You probably assumed I was being skanky and running around with my friend's ex, didn't you?" She eyeballed all three of us, her hands fixed on her hips, eyes squinted while she waited for an answer.

"We didn't think that," Atlas said, lying badly.

Dayton pursed her lips. "Umm. Hmm."

"Well, I applaud your efforts, but we are not play-acting the television show *To Catch a Predator*. As you saw tonight, this situation is dangerous," I warned them.

"We had to do something," Callie said, blowing out a long breath that caught a wisp of her hair before it landed softly against her cheek. She was distracting me without even trying. No wonder the ex was stalking us.

"We caught him putting the drugs he planned to use in a little secret compartment in his belt buckle," I told them, without telling them where we were when we saw him do it.

"You guys were spying on him?" Callie asked, and I couldn't tell what emotion was radiating from her wide eyes.

"Yes, we were. You didn't think I'd sit back and do nothing knowing what he almost did to you," I reminded her.

Her eyes gleamed with surprise and a hint of pride. She wasn't upset, but stress lines remained on her forehead.

"Now, that's what I'm talking about. A man willing to do what the hell it takes to protect his woman," Dayton shouted out before reaching out her fist to bump mine. Her enthusiastic reaction to my wanting to protect Callie made me chuckle despite the situation.

"I appreciate you defending my honor, but I don't want any of you getting hurt any further because I made a bad choice in a man," Callie said. A heavy coat of tension rode her body hard enough to make her slump in defeat.

I lowered to a stooping position before her, rubbing the side of her leg when I noticed how concerned she was about our safety. She was directly affected by this, so I could imagine the level of stress she was dealing with, all while maintaining a highly demanding job.

My words were meant only for her, but the silence in the room let me know that all ears were wide open.

"Baby. I can't call myself *your* man if I can't protect you. Tonight wasn't exactly how we planned it, but by no means am I giving up."

"We.." Atlas corrected me.

"What he said," Ransome added.

A relieved breath filled my lungs, and pride warmed my heart. How did I get so lucky to have friends willing to dance on the fringes of breaking the law to help me? The way this situation was unfolding, laws were protecting a sexual predator, and we were left to navigate a way around them to expose him.

"*We* are by no means giving up. Donni has to be dealt with. I've come across men like him before. I've had to dance beside men like him. Men like him keep pushing until they get what he wants by any means necessary or until they hurt or even kill someone," I said, allowing my eyes to meet every alert pair in the room.

"How are we supposed to stop him?" Callie asked. "I went back to the precinct to speak with the police yesterday. My case is not even a case. I, we...." She glanced up at her friends. "We challenged them to pull my report, and they couldn't even find it. That's how seriously they're taking what happened to me. Said it was probably on someone's desk, that they have to handle the most deadly cases first. It's why we felt the need to come up with a plan to get Donni to slip up and say something or even find a way to sneak into his house to find evidence."

I jerked back at the notion before my head shook. My eyes fell closed at the idea of something bad happening to her.

"You..." I paused to glance at her friends. "None of you can risk your lives like that. What if he caught you? Does he have a gun or guns? What if he drugged you and…" I couldn't finish the sentence. This shit was a high-octane situation, and all we had was low-grade fuel right now.

Atlas continued to pace, tapping the side of his head like it would magically produce the answer. Dayton aimed a finger at him, but her eyes were on me. "Is he going to be alright? You'd think that Callie was his woman or something?"

"On his day job, he gets paid to think, so it bothers the shit out of him when he's faced with a problem he can't solve right away."

Dayton's eyes narrowed and bounced back and forth between me and a more aggressively pacing Atlas. There was a question in her expression that I couldn't answer. I'd already slipped and said too much of my friend's business.

"I have an idea," Callie said, drawing our attention. It was all that stopped Atlas from pacing a hole in my floor. "Donni is only going to respond to aggression. We have to beat him at his own game. Instead of trying to catch him in the act or get him to slip up and say something incriminating, maybe we can find a way to use the drugs on him that he's been using on women?"

Inquisitive brows lifted, and I wasn't sure if I liked how far she was willing to go to get her ex.

"Those date rape drugs, when used in the right dosage, can also be used as a truth serum, can't they?" Callie asked.

These women weren't the damsel in distress types. They were talking about breaking into the man's house and drugging him.

"No. They are two different types of drugs," Ransome answered her question.

"We should still use his own weapons against him," Dayton suggested. I believed Dayton would be the one most likely to hop in her car, drive over to his place, and torture a confession out of him.

I loved the idea of using Donni's own drugs against him, but I didn't want them to know how far I was willing to go, so I shrugged, feigning indifference.

Callie and Charlene glanced at each other before locking gazes with Dayton. There was some type of girl vibe I didn't understand passing between them.

Ransome's gaze was lost in the space of the wall before him, and I could tell by his determined posture that he was contemplating Callie's suggestion. Atlas stood staring at the ceiling with a finger under his chin.

"You may be on to something," I finally added. "We'll have to research on what, how much, and the effects. I would like to stress that what we are discussing isn't legal, but given that the system is giving this man a pass, this idea might be our only option," I finished.

My gaze locked with Callie's while all types of scenarios continued to churn in my head.

"Does he have another residence? One that they don't film his Internet show at?"

A smile flashed in her gaze. "Yes, and I know the address."

Were we about to embark on a situation that would land us all in jail, or were we about to stop a predator from taking advantage of more women?

Chapter Twenty-one

Callie

Two hours later.

After everyone had left, Trent relaxed on the couch, and I settled against him, my head laying against his chest. The six of us had drilled our plan to take down Donni so deeply into our heads that I'd gotten a headache.

Trent was being macho about his injuries. His ego wasn't as inflated as my ex's, but he wanted no part in me feeling sorry for him despite his bruises. If anything, it appeared he was proud to wear them as a representation of him defending my honor.

"You think this plan of ours is going to work?"

"I know it's going to work. This time, we're all on the same page," he replied.

"I agree. With all of us working together, we should be able to take him down."

He stood, reaching down for me, and I eagerly took his hand. The gleam in his eyes was saying that our strategy talks were done.

Good.

He didn't pull me up—he snatched my ass up, making my chest collide with his. My gasp was crushed between our lips, him lavishing mine with a fevered kiss. He didn't care about bruises or the soreness that I was sure coursed through his body after the brutal club fight. He was all about what was about to go down in his living room because neither of us appeared ready to stop this heat from getting hotter.

"Although it has been a stressful, sort of strange and confrontational day, I've had you on the brain all damn day," he said huskily.

"You have?" I asked playfully before I reached down and ran my hand down the length of his dick that was pressed firmly against those pants.

"What if I told you that all I've been thinking about all day is having this masterpiece..." I gave it a light squeeze, making him shiver. "...Slamming all the way to the back of my pussy. You know, those hard-to-reach areas that you don't have a problem getting to?"

He reached down, hand gripping and squeezing my ass before he dropped them lower and gripped my hips. He lifted, dragging me up his body with ease so my legs wrapped around his waist.

"I know those places *very* well, and if that is where you want me to go, then that is where I'll be getting to in a moment. The only question I have for you is..."

He kissed me, crushing his lips into mine again for another fiery session of our tongues exploring and eager mouths tasting while he ground his length into me. The firm pressure teased my clit, making me leak shamelessly into my panties.

"What's the question?" I asked breathlessly, eager to know.

"How fucking hard do you want it? You want me to beat up those hard-to-reach places, or do you want me to tease them?"

"Mmm," I moaned, getting off on this slow grind he was gifting me with and this pre-sex discussion we were having.

"I want you to beat it so good that the only way I'll be able to sit is on a lean."

At those words, he turned my ass loose and worked his strong hand along my thighs, lowering me. My legs slid down his body, pussy getting dragged along the front of him until my feet touched down light on the floor. It was like he was being delicate in preparation for what we'd discussed.

I helped him out of his shirt, not caring about the damage I caused to his buttons when I caught the two halves at his chest and snatched it wide open. He didn't give a shit about that shirt because his tongue slid between my bra-covered tits while he worked my shirt up and off my arms.

I ripped his belt loose, twisted open his button, and, like his shirt, I gripped the open halves of his pants and snatched them open, likely breaking the zipper.

He bent, stopping me from doing my job when he grabbed my jeans. He yanked hard, snatching my pants open with a *thump*.

Wiggling to help him, he damn near ripped me from my jeans like I had done his. They zipped down my legs once he worked them over my ass. The jeans were tossed like discarded paper once my feet were cleared.

He didn't resume his standing position. He stayed down there while I stood above him with my legs slightly parted. His gaze was pinned on my pussy. All that stood between us were my panties, which I'm sure were soaked through.

"Give me these. They're in the damn way," he said, snatching my panties clean off like they were nothing but a paper cutout draped over me. He gripped my waist and turned me slightly.

"Left foot on the couch," he commanded. He didn't have to tell me twice. I lifted my leg quickly, flashing him all my dripping glory. His tongue licked across his lips a few times before he glanced up, flashing me a look I didn't know how to read.

I choked out a scream because his face, mouth, and tongue were immediately buried in my pussy. I gripped two hands full of silky dark brown hair to keep my balance. He was doing everything in his power to give me a tongue-lashing that was tailor-made to make me come.

Shit," I whimpered, my breaths out of control, my chest heavy, my legs starting to shake. What the hell kind of magical tricks was this man doing down there?

He glanced up, rolling his tongue across his lips in a way that made it look like a dance move.

"Best fucking thing to ever come across my tongue," he said before he went back to work. He continued dancing tongue strokes on my pussy. The raw pleasure of it had me choking on sharp gasps. It was almost too much.

"Ho. Ly. Fuck," came out as three words instead of two when the building intensity consumed me. Trent was performing a miracle on my clit that in the past was sluggish and limp but now pulsed with life and perked up with pride and joy.

"Fucking coming," flew out of my mouth in a hot rush of elongated words. My face squinted tightly, my hands squeezed tighter with his silky hair slipping between my fingers, and my lower half thrusted into his face.

It was too soon for me to be teetering on the edge of my desire, but I couldn't stop this raw, unwavering flow. It was so damn delicious. The high that ripped through me could never be duplicated. The hypnotic surge of tremors swept me up in waves of cresting sensations that enveloped me in delicious satisfaction.

"Mmh," was all I could squeeze out while I fought not to nod off.

Damn!

I managed to peel open my tightly squeezed eyes to see Trent smirking up at me. He made a show of running his mystical tongue across his lips after passing it through the juices that had leaked down my legs.

The leg he'd insisted I prop up on the couch was too heavy to lift now, so I dragged it down and let it drop to the floor like a heavy stone. Weak-legged, weak-kneed, and weak-bodied, my heavy gaze still managed to track Trent's movements.

He came out of those pants and boxer briefs in a graceful flash. He'd mastered the art of stripping away his clothing as quickly as possible. This was one occasion I was glad he possessed the fast-maneuvering ability. When he sat on the couch, my head jerked at his positioning, my question resting in the deep crease of my forehead.

"What? What are you doing? Aren't you going to manhandle me and jerk me around like you did the last time?"

Damn, that was supposed to stay in my head. He didn't need to know I liked it rough. However, there was no way that he'd not already figured out I got off on the way he handled me. Asking him the question out loud made his already hard dick rise to a proud full salute.

He nodded at my questions, the smirk on his face wicked.

"Trust me, baby, just because you're going to be riding doesn't mean you're going to be driving. Now, climb your sexy ass on and prepare to be fucked."

Oh yes!

I didn't climb aboard—it was more like jumping through the air and landing on his lap. My damp thighs landed against his, making a loud, slapping noise that made it sound like we were already fucking.

Like synced souls, we drew closer for a hot kiss. This time, it was delicate, our lips fusing at the perfect angle and pressure to allow raw, unchecked emotions to creep into the scene.

"I like this," I mouthed against his lips. He eased back as his fire-lit gaze scanned me and burned hot enough to make my breath catch. He caught a lock of my hair and twirled it around his finger.

"Me too. It's like being in the eye of the storm. Quiet, peaceful, and very deceitful because we know this calm will be followed up by a vicious downpour. Don't we?"

I swallowed a big lump of lust, nodding my agreement before I took another kiss to calm my pulsing lady parts. The light stroke of his fingers up my side and back left chill bumps in their wake and had me gritting my teeth to fight a shiver.

His tongue had its own mind and was damn near down my throat when he began to lift me, forcing me to place my hands on his shoulders.

I made an attempt to ease back. "No," he whispered, sucking my bottom lip between his. He bit my lip hard enough to leave a sting that was timed perfectly with him letting me drop.

"Oh! Fuck!" I yelled out, not prepared for the deep impact. My poor walls cried for tension relief and, at the same time, cheered for the stretching pleasure that emanated from our deep connection.

He didn't give my clenching core time to adjust as he thrust into me, getting to those hard-to-reach places. In mere seconds, those places wept and applauded his efforts with involuntary movements that only heightened the pleasure.

He kept lifting me up and letting me drop down his length, the pulsing ache sinful. It shot a wickedly devastating pleasure through my core that danced up my body and made me shiver.

"Trent. Trent."

My voice was a mix of a whimper and a cry as he lifted me high above him.

"It's too. It's too—"

Down I went. "Oh my. Fuck!" I shouted so loud I knew I'd be hoarse in the morning. He leaned down and took one of my nipples, gripping it between his teeth, right before he lifted and let me drop again, harder this time. He tugged on my nipple while I cried out from the impact of my repeated rises to the crown of his dick and descending down the thick long shaft.

Breathless, heaving, heart hammering its way out my chest, I clawed up his back and shoulders until my nails slipped off his taunt skin from the way I gripped and pulled like he was a damn comforter.

He kept me in place with a firm arm around my lower back. He was buried so damn deep I was afraid to move and swore I felt him moving in my stomach. He held me as steady as possible while his slow, deep thrust allowed the head to wet my walls down and produce a tension-fulfilling stretch that drove me insane.

Every time I moved, his strong arms tightened around my waist, constricting me to him and making my breathless state that much more intense. Every nerve ending caught fire, and I felt this man all the way up to my damn tingling scalp.

Shaking uncontrollably, my head was a bit twitchy, but I managed to kiss him hard one moment and bite into his neck and shoulder the next. I would have to apologize later for the claw and teeth marks. It couldn't be helped. With this kind of fucking, you had to have something to ground you, or you would eventually combust.

"Trent. Bay-bee, bay-bee," I called out. I'm sure I appeared as drunk as I sounded. He continued to use his dick to tunnel his way into the deepest depths of me. The tingling, the nerve-tickling spikes of pleasure—they were too much and too damn good. All senses ceased to exist, and I shot off like a fire-soaked bullet.

"Oh! Father-God," I cried out. If Trent didn't have a telepathic line to my pussy, my name wasn't Callie.

This was one reason why this man had invaded my damn brain for a whole year. No one else could do me like this, getting me off so damn good that I forgot about everything and everyone. He made the whole world cease to exist.

"Damn, that was…fucking intense," he said, his whisper harsh and breathy. "Your pussy is clamping down around my dick so hard," he added, pushing out the words. I shuddered each time a tremor shot through me and pulsed through my overworked lady parts.

There was no doubt about it. This delicious beatdown would be humming through me tomorrow. I planned to wear comfortable shoes because sitting on my sore kitty was out of the question.

What was I thinking, letting him go that deep and hard? The ache was already knocking on my lady parts because my mind was freakier than my body could handle.

Chapter Twenty-two

Callie

We jolted awake at the same time, my elbow catching Trent in the side in my frenzied need to grasp reality. Our heads lifted, and our bodies followed, darting upright. The shrill yelling of a car alarm had us up and off the bed within seconds.

The lamp snapped on in time for me to spot Trent picking up his T-shirt that he threw over his head in a rush. He followed up with a pair of jeans he snatched off the dresser and yanked up his well-defined legs.

Despite all the deeply impacting sex we'd had on his couch, after we showered together, we'd gotten in another quickie when an innocent goodnight kiss got us all worked up again.

"My car alarm," Trent said, running to his bedroom window to peek out.

I was in one of his T-shirts that fit like a nightgown, with no panties because I'd been ripped out of them when our clothes started coming off.

"Damn it!" he spat, frustrated at the sight of what was happening outside.

He turned back, bent, and snatched something from under his bed before he took off in a dash for the front door.

"What?" I asked, running to the dresser and jumping into a pair of his shorts that swallowed me. I gripped one side of them to keep them from falling back down my legs as I ran after him. He didn't reply.

He snatched the front door open and marched past the small entranceway to his driveway. The solar-powered lights along his hedges illuminated parts of his front yard and allowed me to catch the outline of the gun shoved down the back of his pants.

I didn't know he owned a gun. What the hell was going on? Why would he need a gun in a neighborhood like this? Why would his car alarm be going off in a neighborhood like this?

My anxious eyes swept my surroundings. Lights snapped on inside homes, and window curtains began to move, some shifting gradually apart at the sound of the commotion. Trent silenced his car's alarm, aiming the key fob while his head was on a constant swivel.

"Trent," I called, my tone shaky from the sudden flow of fear flooding my system. I remained in the entryway just outside the front door, gripping one of the two pillars that supported the area.

"Please stay back," Trent called over his shoulder to me while continuing to creep closer to his car, scanning it for damage.

My face creased into a tight knot from my vision pushing through the inky black space in the distance. Was that a car creeping from a dark section of the road?

"Trent, get down!" I yelled before a set of bright headlights snapped on. A car appeared from the darkness, the tires scratching against the road, releasing a sound like a shrieking ghost.

I dived behind a stand of bushes, not that they offered much protection other than to keep me from being seen. When I managed to lift up enough to peek, all I saw was a muzzle flash emanating from the driver's side window of the fast-moving car and Trent going down.

"No!" I cried out, the word ripping from my throat in one long scream.

The screech of tires sounded, and the dark car disappeared like it was an avenging spirit that was never there. I took off, not caring about my own life anymore. I had to get to Trent. Other than my heartbeat pounding in my ears, all other sounds ceased to exist. The neighborhood fell away from my view, my vision tunneling to Trent.

I dropped to his side, scraping my knees on his paved driveway in the process. He was laid out on his side, thankfully, moving.

"Trent. Oh my God. Trent!" I yelled, trying to turn him while frantically searching for bullet holes. When my eyes zeroed in on his chest and the blood wetting his T-shirt and rapidly expanding, I lost a chunk of my sanity to a flood of tears and throat-gripping sobs.

"No. No. Trent. No."

His eyes. They were open. There was movement. Blinks. His breathing, though harsh and erratic, kept me from losing all sense of reality.

"You're going to be okay," I promised him in a tone that didn't match my current state of mind. Help. He needed help. He needed me to do whatever I could to stop his bleeding. I placed my hand atop the now-soaked area of his chest, the liquid warm, wet, and visually terrifying.

He struggled to turn, coughing and gasping while his body shook involuntarily. I couldn't let him go into shock.

"Lie still. Please!" I begged. My throat jumped from a series of hard swallows when I inhaled the rusted scent of his blood. I had to keep it together. I had to help.

Think.

Think.

I kept reminding myself to think, but my brain was misfiring. Too many thoughts. Too much fear.

His phone found its way to my free hand, or maybe I had found it in the midst of my panic. I didn't know. I swiped the screen several times before the face illuminated. Thank every deity known, his phone wasn't locked.

"Lie still, baby. I need to see the wound," I told him, lifting his shirt with his phone pinned between my ear and shoulder.

"I'm. I can…" he stuttered and struggled to lift himself, but I pressed a firm hand down on his shoulder to keep him in place. Every time he moved, the blood stain expanded, getting wetter and spreading wider.

"You have to lie still for me, baby, please," I begged, although I knew what I was asking was almost impossible.

"9-1-1, what's your emergency?" The greeting sounded in my ear.

"My boyfriend has been shot. Please send someone to 214 Hayward Court," I said, my words rushed and choppy. My hard sniffing and frantic search for the source of blood made me lose control of the phone, but I caught it before it dropped to the ground.

"Where is he shot?" the female operator asked.

"Upper chest area. He's bleeding out. I can't find the source to stop the bleeding. Please send someone fast," I begged the woman like she controlled how fast emergency responders could make it to us.

He groaned, and pain emanated from the sound, causing the hair on my arms to stand. Frustration, fear, and anger were at war inside me. I couldn't find the damn hole.

My hand moved carefully while my fingers slipped over the bloodstained skin of his chest. Trent groaned again, and this time, it was followed up by a sickening wheeze when he inhaled.

"Apply pressure to the wound and do your best to stop the bleeding. I've dispatched a unit that should be there in about ten minutes."

Ten minutes was an eternity when the person you loved was lying in his own driveway, bleeding out. My palm glided across an area that was slightly rougher and jagged. Was it torn flesh?

"Keep the line open until help arrives," the woman said, but I didn't reply. I was too busy leaning down to see if I had found the wound.

Trent lifted his hand and caught my wrist in his weak grip, forcing me to look at him. His face had gone so pale, the pain etched in his expression palpable.

"Use the light on the phone," he blew the words out in a harsh whisper before he sucked in another wheezing breath. I wiped my hands on his shirt that I wore before I swiped the phone's dark surface to turn on the phone's flashlight. My fingers slipped across the glass, leaving smeared prints, but I managed to tap the light on.

"Is everything all right?" a voice sounded behind me, causing me to damn near jump out of my skin. A white couple appeared in my back view. The neighbors, I supposed. The woman clutched the front halves of her robe even though it was tied tightly around her waist.

"I was a medic when I was in the military. I can help," the man stated.

Finally, I shone the light on Trent's chest.

"We need to stop the bleeding," the man who once was a medic stated the obvious. "May I?" he asked.

"Yes. Please help him. I can't find the entry wound. I can't stop the bleeding," I cried my shaky words to the man.

"Trent," I whispered. The light shook in my hands so badly, it appeared Trent had a disco ball hanging above him.

"I found the entry wound," the man said. "I need a piece of plastic. Grace, go and get the plastic wrap. Fast, baby. Hurry."

The woman took off while I kneeled next to Trent, shining a light where blood poured from his chest wound like it was an open spicket. The neighbor did a quick check, ensuring that there weren't any more wounds.

"I need to turn you a little. I need to see if there's an exit wound," the former medic told Trent.

Trent nodded, his teeth sinking deep into his bottom lip, pain registering in every part of his body and pouring from his eyes and facial expression.

"No exit wound," the man said, speaking his thoughts out loud. I didn't know what that meant and was too afraid to ask. He returned Trent to his back, and hearing his whimpers tore at my heart.

Blood continued to gush from the wound, the sight making me swallow hard and fast. My tears wouldn't ease up and only allowed me to see Trent through a series of blurry and clear snapshots.

When the neighbor took his pointer finger and jammed it into the hole, my jaw dropped. All I could do was stare from the man to the wound and to a pain-sickened Trent.

"My name's Carlye," he introduced himself to Trent.

"T-t-rent," Trent muttered, his name barely discernible, his voice weak. Even in the dim lighting, I noticed him growing paler. His bottom lip trembled, the sight adding enough weight to my mental anxiety I was afraid I'd snap at any moment. My grip on his hand would give him another wound to worry about if I didn't ease up.

"You're going to be okay," I assured him, hoping it wasn't a lie. Our relationship had barely begun. We'd hardly had any time to enjoy each other, to get to know each other. Add the petty antics of my ex-boyfriend and our time together had been marred by so much outside interference it was a wonder we hadn't gone insane by now.

The slipper-clad footsteps of Carlye's wife grew closer. When she was near enough to us, she began to pull apart the plastic, ripping off a piece and handing it to her husband. He removed his finger and replaced it with the thin sheet of plastic wrap, shoving the material into the wound.

The distant sound of sirens relieved more of my anxiety, but Trent's hand had gone so cold inside mine that it chilled me down to the bone. I lifted and placed a delicate kiss on his cold hand.

"You're going to be okay."

I made myself believe the words I was forcing from my mouth. I couldn't lose Trent. Not now. We had so much life to live together—so much more to discover about each other.

A squad car rolled up, followed by a fire truck, and right on its trail was an ambulance. As soon as the ambulance pulled to a stop, the back door popped open, and the medics and the gurney hit the ground at the same time. The team from the ambulance, along with one from the fire truck, ran in our direction, carrying their equipment and wheeling the gurney.

The neighbor backed off, and although it took great effort, I let go of Trent's hands to allow the medics to do their jobs.

"Sucking chest wound. Collapsed lung," Carlye relayed to the medics. There was so much equipment and packages being ripped open, and the way they turned Trent so effortlessly while coaching him through what they did was impressive. It's funny you don't appreciate another person's job or knowledge until you see them in action.

It took me a moment to snap out of my trance to hear the operator calling out to me.

"Yes," I answered. "They're here. Thank you," I said, clicking off.

A light tap on my shoulder made me jump. It was the neighbor's wife.

"Go and get dressed so you can go with him. Carlye and I will keep an eye on Trent's house when you leave," she said, leaning in to be discreet with her words. Trent's neighbors were a blessing I was grateful for.

I nodded, gripping the waistband of Trent's big shorts and his gun that I was hiding under them when I took an unsteady step back. I hated to leave him for even a moment, but there was no way I wasn't going with him. After a few shaky steps back, I marched toward the house before taking off running.

"Ma'am. Ma'am," someone said, calling me, I presumed. A quick glance, and I found one of the cops waving after me. Had he seen Trent's gun? I wasn't waiting around to see. I kept it moving like I didn't hear him.

Once I was back in the bedroom, I shoved Trent's gun deep under the mattress. I tugged off the shirt and shorts and jumped into my clothes before grabbing my purse. While running back to the front door, I fished around inside my purse for my phone and dialed Dayton. She answered on the first ring.

"Hello."

"Trent's been shot. The paramedics are working on him and preparing to take him to the hospital."

Due to my hasty movements and cracked words, I wasn't sure if she understood me.

"What? Wait. Slow down. Did you say Trent's been shot?"

"Yes. They are about to take him to the ambulance now. I'm going with him. He was shot in his driveway," I relayed, my words, a speedy barrage of merging syllables I wasn't sure made sense.

"What the whole entire fuck? Is he going to be okay? Where was he shot? What hospital are they taking him to?" Dayton questioned.

"Ma'am, my name is Detective Glover with the RVPD. Can I ask you a few questions about what happened here tonight?" One of the cops was on the prowl like they were actually going to do anything.

I must have nodded because he proceeded with his questions.

"What are your names?"

"I'm Callie Hendrix, and the victim is Trenton Pierce," I managed to say without sobbing.

The man asked a few other random questions about me and Trent. I supplied quick, thoughtless answers. I lifted my phone to my ear when I realized Dayton yelling to get my attention.

"Dayton," I said, answering her frantic shouts for answers.

"What happened here tonight?" the cop asked, cutting me off. He didn't care about me or my phone conversation.

"We were sleeping. His car alarm sounded. He went out to check and…" I released a pent-up cry that sounded more like a shout before I sucked in a sharp breath, trying to gather myself.

"Callie! Callie! Are you okay? What the fuck is happening?" Dayton yelled into the phone, desperate to find out what had happened. The cop blocking my pathway back to Trent made the ache in my heart intensify. I peeked around the man's broad shoulder in time to see the medics gearing up to move Trent into the ambulance.

Flashing lights lit up the otherwise quiet neighborhood, and for the first time, I took in the sight of more of Trent's neighbors. A few stood in their driveways, and others were huddled together on the side of the street, narrating to others what they believed had happened.

In this neighborhood, this type of violence was almost unheard of. Even if it wasn't his fault, I wouldn't be surprised if they petitioned to get Trent kicked out. I glanced at the cop, picking up the last part of another question.

"His car. He came to check the alarm. He. When."

A hard swallow and deep inhale helped me gather myself. I pointed to where they lifted the gurney before lifting my pity-filled eyes to the cop.

"I have to go with him. Please," I begged.

"Okay, a few more questions, and I'll let you go, but you have to come in and give a formal statement. You said he left to check on his car alarm, and what happened after that?"

"Um. Um," I said. My words were all jumbled up in my head.

"He was walking down the driveway, and a car came from out of nowhere, and someone just shot him."

The cop said something, but I was too distracted to translate his words. I nodded with my eyes glued to the medics with Trent. The second cop was questioning Trent's neighbors, Carlye and Grace.

"We'll be in touch, Ms. Hendrix. I also want to hear about this club fight Mr. Pierce got into earlier tonight."

How the hell did he know about that already? I didn't respond. I had too much going on to play twenty-one questions with the cops. I stepped around him, lifted the phone to my ear, and resumed talking to Dayton, who sounded like an auction announcer, her voice came through the phone so loud.

"He was…shot. In the…." I ran alongside the moving gurney. "In the chest."

"Fuck!" Dayton shouted. "Is he…"

"He's alive. I have to go."

"What hospital are they taking him to?" she questioned.

"I'll text you the hospital. I gotta go," I said, clicking off in time to follow the medics and Trent into the back of the ambulance.

Chapter Twenty-three

Callie

I paced, took a seat, and then hopped right back up. I nibbled on my short acrylic nails. Sat, stood, and paced again. I was a raging mess of nerves and unspent energy.

It had only been thirty minutes, but it felt like days had passed since the announcement of Trent going into emergency surgery. They had to remove the bullet and mitigate the damage to his collapsed lung.

The pain he must be in. All of that blood. The agony I recalled seeing on his stressed face. His eyes had been begging for mercy, and I was helpless to do anything to take his pain away. Like now, all I could do was pray and wait.

"Callie." I turned at the sound of my name. It was Dayton and Atlas, and a few paces behind them were Ransome and Charlene.

I ran into Dayton's arms, needing her embrace more than I imagined. Charlene joined, throwing her arms around the both of us.

"How is he?"

"Is he okay?"

They asked their questions into my hair while in our huddle. I eased back, the movement causing them to loosen their grip on me until we separated. Two sets of stressed eyes were locked on me, as worried about me as they were about Trent.

"They took him into emergency surgery. From what the doctor explained, it sounded more like multiple surgeries. One to remove the bullet and one to fix his collapsed lung. They wouldn't tell me if he would be okay. If he's lost too much blood. If he'll make a full recovery or not. Nothing."

My hands lifted in helpless surrender, my neck collapsing into my shoulders.

"He's going to be fine," Charlene assured, squeezing my arm and keeping her warm hand wrapped around it. My eyes found the floor, the weight of them as heavy as the emotional turmoil wreaking havoc on me.

I lifted my gaze when I sensed eyes on me. Atlas and Ransome stood quietly observing us. I reached out a hand to the men, and they took cautious steps closer to our little circle.

"I was able to get in touch with his mother. She has to fly in from California and won't make it here until tomorrow," Atlas said.

Hearing him mention Trent's mother spoke for the newness of our relationship. He'd mentioned his mother on several occasions but glossed over the parts about them having a tough time when he was growing up. His mother, or more so the way he'd grown up, was a subject he wasn't ready to go into details about, so I didn't press him.

I had overheard him speaking to her on the phone. Based on his side of the conversation, and the positive way in which he spoke to her, I would venture to say that they got along relatively well.

We hadn't gotten to the phase in our relationship where we met family. Now that Trent's mother was on the way, how was I supposed to introduce myself to her when it was my fault Trent had been shot in the first place?

"Let's sit," Ransome suggested, breaking apart the torturous ideas stomping around in my head like a college marching band.

Positive vibes, I kept repeating in my head. Trent was strong. He would fight. He would survive this.

A reminder of how he'd ended up here and who may have shot him kept me in a constant state of paranoia. Nervous energy buzzed in my ears and wouldn't let up. I kept relentlessly dredging up horrific images of death and destruction.

Why had Trent been shot? Who shot him? Where were they now? What if they showed up at the hospital to finish the job? Should I have asked the cops to protect Trent while he was here?

"I'll go and get us some coffee," Atlas volunteered.

Charlene and Dayton sat on either side of me, one placing a caring hand on the side of my shoulder, the other placing it on my shaking leg. I kept releasing long breaths for no reason while eye-balling the entryway that led into this waiting room. All I wanted most in this moment was for the doctor to materialize with good news.

At the sight of someone approaching, my breath caught and released fast until I noticed it was Atlas returning with coffee and donuts. He displayed the food and beverages on the coffee table in front of us with condiments and had even managed to find a stack of small disposable plates.

"Thank you. That was thoughtful," I told him. He nodded, swiped a cup of coffee and a donut, and took a seat. My leg resumed shaking when I didn't have something to focus my attention on. Hands on either side of me landed on my leg to keep me from tapping a hole in the floor.

My heart dropped through the floor at the sight of the doctor approaching, but I managed to stand on shaky legs.

His unreadable expression had me ready to yell for him to put me out of my misery.

He stood before our group, staring across the expanse of us, with his hands cupped in front of him. My nerves felt like they were being raked across broken glass with each second that ticked by without him saying anything.

"Mr. Pierce is in recovery. The bullet was removed successfully. But, it perforated his lung, and we had to perform a thoracoscopy surgery for his pneumothorax."

No one responded or said a word. I understood the first part of the doctor's statement. They had successfully removed the bullet. However, the second part was all doctor talk. The tight pull between our eyes and our dazed looks must have clued the doctor in that we couldn't translate the line of syllables he had strung together and called a sentence.

"We closed off the air leakage in his lung and minimized the damage. He will be under close observation in our intensive care unit, but I foresee him making a full recovery in six to eight weeks."

We breathed. Tight shoulders dropped, and breaths released around toothy smiles.

A chorus of cheers erupted from our group, my laughter mingling with the other joy-filled cries in the room.

"Thank you, doctor. Thank you so much. Can I see him? Can we see him? Can I stay here in the hospital with him?" I pleaded with my eyes. "So he won't be here alone," I added.

The doctor's tight expression relaxed a little. "It will be at least another thirty minutes. He's in a fragile state, so only one visitor at a time for short periods. You can stay with him, but you have to let him rest so he can heal," he warned. He kept his eyes pinned on mine to make sure I heeded his warning before he turned and stepped away.

I glanced up at the ceiling and closed my eyes.

Thank you, God.

Chapter Twenty-four

Trent

My consciousness swam. Flashes of images came and went. A familiar face. A sad cry. Pain. It was like being cast out to sea with nothing to keep me afloat. I reached out and grasped a hold of the pieces of my fractured memories, hoping to piece together a moment, a scene, a time.

A firestorm of ideas broke loose, and impressions of moments clapped into my head. The ache of my raging thoughts evoked a physical response. I squeezed my eyes tightly to quiet the storm, but my thoughts wouldn't be still for long enough for me to interpret a single one.

Was it today, tonight, or yesterday that I last saw my friends? *Callie?* Wasn't I just with her? Why was I a mixed-up bowl of soup, my ideas swirling as if being stirred with a spoon?

After an unspecified amount of time passed, things began to calm and come into focus. My eyes fluttered before they sprang open, straining against the light. This wasn't my bedroom.

My head jerked around. Big mistake. I huffed a breath in an attempt to alleviate my pain and released it on a shaky breath. The ache shooting through me almost made my damn bowels release.

Where the hell was I? It didn't take but a few seconds for the tubes running from me to various machines and the constant beep to reveal my location.

Hospital.
Shot.
Drive by.
Callie!

My eyes shot around frantically until they dropped to her sleeping form on the couch on the left side of my bed in front of the wide window. The twinkling city lights peeked in past the thin drapes in the window.

A deep sigh of relief at the knowledge that Callie was safe left my aching chest burning and in pain, but it was worth it to my baby.

How long have I been here?

The date on the monitor was June 29th, which meant it was the same night as my shooting. Who the hell shot me? The only person that came to mind was Callie's ex-boyfriend. Had this been payback for the fight in the club? Did the police know?

The club had been reluctant to call the police, but after this, we had to report what happened. What if Donni's actions had killed me? What if he goes after Callie next?

I needed to make some calls. I needed to talk to somebody. I needed to do something. Anything.

I turned, and my body moved. However, the explosion of pain coursing through me caused me to cry out.

"Oh. Shit. Shit. Shit." I sipped in quick puffs of air.

"Trent, baby. What are you doing? You can't get up," Callie warned. I hadn't seen her get up. Her soft voice didn't match the level of concern expressed on her face. She adjusted my covers while rubbing a soothing hand along my cheek. Her touch was worth the spikes of pain coursing through me.

She was an angel. My angel. And I would walk through hell itself before I let her crazy ex lay a hand on her.

She placed a sweet kiss on my forehead, being careful not to jostle me.

"Thank you for not leaving me. You are the best thing to happen to me in a long time," she said, the sentiment of her words warming my heart.

"You too. I love you," I replied.

Her lips fell apart on a silent 'o' before a smile lit up her face.

"I love you, too," she replied without hesitation.

Leaning closer, she pressed her forehead lightly against mine before she placed a soft kiss on my lips. This time, I didn't let her pull away. I lifted my heavy arm and moved my hand behind her head to keep her in place until I got a real kiss—one that had me getting hard as a damn brick despite the pain radiating through the rest of me.

She filled in the gaps I couldn't remember about the shooting like how the detective already knew about the club fight. It was odd since the club owner was adamant about not alerting the authorities.

Whoever snitched to the cops must have reported the fight before I was shot because the cops knew about the incident before they questioned Callie.

"I have to leave for a few hours tomorrow to meet with Twisted Minds. They have an interview and performance with a late-night talk show. I have an assistant who I've trained, so I'm meeting with her and the group to inform them I won't be able to go to New York."

"But…" She lifted a hand to shut me up. Her strained expression said I better not let the words in my head cross my lips.

"Don't. I'm not leaving this city until you are discharged from this hospital. And I don't want to hear any backtalk about it," she chastised me, knowing what I was about to suggest.

"Okay, ma'am. I won't say a thing. Thank you."

A deep smile spread across my face. How did I get so damned lucky?

"Your mother is flying in. Atlas is picking her up from the airport in the morning."

I hadn't considered the impact this would have on my mother, and if left up to me, I wouldn't have told her until after I was home and healed. I was sure that Atlas was the one who'd called her. Since he was the oldest in our group, he liked to take on the big brother role.

He was the one person in my life who I could never be mad at, even when he pissed me off. Atlas had always been there for me. Even when I was fucking up, he would talk me off the ledge and keep me from falling back into the dark abyss called addiction. The fact that Callie accepted me freely, knowing my past demons, was a blessing that I vowed to never take for granted.

***

My awakening this timed was much smoother. The empty couch caught my attention. *Callie.*

The tension in my shoulders eased when I remembered her mentioning meeting with her assistant and the group.

The door to my room snapped open, making me jump. The nurse came in reading something from a clipboard before she glanced up with a friendly smile.

"You know I'm going to ask the obvious question, Mr. Pierce," she paused to read more from my chart before glancing up. "How are you feeling?"

I returned a smile, fighting not to grimace in the process.

"Some aches and some pains, but I'm grateful to be alive."

It was a lie, as it felt like I'd been put through a meat grinder. She went about the business of checking my vitals, and I fought not to wince at every action. She noticed and gave me a reassuring smile.

"I know you specifically requested to be taken off your pain meds because of your past battle with addiction, but we can administer doses that are safe."

I shook my head at her suggestion.

"Those were dark times, and I'd rather deal with the pain than allow something like that to stake its claim on my life again."

She took out a needle filled with a white liquid.

"I just...don't know about taking anything."

"It's not pain meds. It's antibiotics to keep away unwanted infections. This is perfectly safe."

I stared at her without answering, stressed about receiving medicine I didn't know how to verify.

Once she was done, the nurse patted my leg and left without another word.

She wasn't wearing a nametag? I didn't know what she'd given me. Why was the heavy hands drowsiness suddenly dragging me down? What the hell was hap...pen...ing?

Chapter Twenty-five

Callie

The meeting with my assistant and Twisted Minds had gone well. After making sure they had everything they needed and back up just in case, they wished me well with hugs and kisses.

I strolled back into the hospital, grateful that Trent was alive, and even managed to hold on to a genuine smile. Detective Glover had called and left me a message, but I ignored it, not in the mood to deal with him yet.

"Where is he? They told me he was in room 705. He's not there!" The woman at the counter was clearly agitated, her leg jumping and her hand tapping lightly against the top of the counter in the hopes of making the nurse at the desk work faster to provide her answers.

705?

That was Trent's room. The woman didn't look much older than me. I prayed it wasn't one of Trent's exes. I was too stressed to hold my peace if it were.

He'd had an *active* past with women that he was open and honest with me about. Although I was the so-called quiet type based on other people's opinions of me, I wasn't timid enough to be someone's fool. It's why I'd walked away from my ex in the first place.

Maybe the woman had gotten the number wrong. I ran past her while she continued to demand answers from the nurse. I tore through Trent's door only to find the room empty. The blanket and pillow Dayton and Charlene had brought me last night remained folded neatly on the couch where I'd left them two and a half hours ago.

Stay calm, I reminded myself.

This was a hospital. They took patients to run tests, collect urine, and do things like take X-rays. They could have been performing any number of tasks with Trent.

My temporary moment of self-motivative insight didn't stop me from turning in a circle like the universe itself would give me answers. All of the equipment was there, but the IVs and tubes were thrown about, some left hanging from the machines.

I ended up at the same desk as the woman I'd just run past.

"He was checked out and taken to another facility. Here's all the paperwork. It was signed off by our chief medical officer," the nurse explained, handing the woman a clipboard full of paperwork.

"Is that information for Trenton Pierce?" I asked, snatching both women's attention.

The nurse lifted a brow without answering, bringing the clipboard to her chest to prevent me from seeing the information. Was she unaware that I'd been with him since he was admitted? Did these people not communicate with each other?

"Are you Callie?" The woman standing next to me asked, looking me up and down. I didn't miss the edge to her tone.

"Yes," I answered reluctantly, one brow stuck in the air.

"I'm Martina Pierce, Trent's mother." She pointed a stiff finger at the nurse behind the glass partition, who pretended to be busy searching for more paperwork. "This ditsy-ass nurse is trying to tell me that they let someone check Trent out of this hospital."

"What? Who?" I asked her, stunned by the update on Trent and about who she was. Martina was short in stature with long dark hair that she swept up into a neat ponytail. I could tell right away that she was feisty. Her light, hazel-green eyes matched Trent's so perfectly there was no mistaking they were mother and son.

"Wait until you hear this shit?" Martina, who appeared too young to be Trent's mother, began. "They are saying his brother checked him out to upgrade him to a better hospital."

I didn't understand.

"We have all the proper paperwork," the nurse stated, looking terrified.

"Trent doesn't…"

"…Have a brother," Martina finished my statement. "I'd definitely know if I pushed out a second child. After almost dying at fourteen to have him, do you think I was fool enough to go running to have another?"

That explained why she looked so young.

"What did this supposed brother look like?" she asked the nurse while drumming her fingers atop the counter, waiting for an answer that made sense.

The woman's eyes rocked back and forth between me and Martina.

"I'll call my supervisor to come and speak to you," the nurse finally said, cracking under the heat of our stares and hurriedly picking up the phone.

***

An hour later.

Martina and I were about one loud complaint away from being kicked out of the hospital. The staff had fucked up and released Trent on paperwork that was supposedly signed by the hospital's chief medical officer.

However, the chief medical officer was adamant that he had not signed release papers. The hospital listed on the paperwork wasn't one that he recognized, so he assumed it was a private facility.

What the hell is going on?

It was the thousandth time the question had gone off in my head as well as being asked out loud to the hospital staff. Atlas and Ransome had shown up to see Trent and added their fuel to the fire upon finding out about the situation.

Trent's mother, along with Atlas, threatened to sue the hospital, everyone in it, and their families. The threats held enough weight for the hospital to get the authorities involved to investigate what happened.

Atlas attempted to convince them to allow us access to the surveillance footage to see who had taken Trent, but they were legally bound to only release that type of information to the proper authorities.

Now, we were back in the same waiting room, the day after Trent had been shot, waiting for the authorities to come in and figure out who'd moved him and why. I prayed that this was an internal mistake and he'd been accidentally transferred to another hospital.

"This shit is straight off a soap opera," Martina said. "I mean, who takes a whole grown ass man from the hospital and no one not know who it was and where the hell they went?"

I shrugged. If my shoulders got any heavier and if my head pounded any harder, I feared I would have to be admitted to the hospital myself.

"Let me at least officially introduce myself," Martina said, reaching out a hand to me. I took it.

"Martina Pierce. I wish we could have met under better conditions. Trent has told me so much about you. I feel like I already know you."

"He has?" My eyes widened at the notion that she already knew about me.

"He told me about you the first time you two met in New York. I told him then that you were the one, but the fool ass boy he was didn't listen to me."

How was I supposed to respond? The knowledge that Trent's mother already knew about last year left me speechless. Did she know that we met on what was supposed to be a one-night stand hook-up?

"Wow," I finally choked out. After New York, Trent and I had never spoken again for a year because he'd left my number when he left me at that hotel. It was all the message that I'd needed at the time that we were a blip of happiness that would forever be lost in that time and space. Him telling his mother about me was further proof that he believed we were more than a fling.

"Now," she said, saving me from having to scramble for something else to say. "If these people don't find my son, there's going to be hell to pay. How can you transfer a patient and not know the damned transfer location or who did the transporting? The shit sounds fishy to me."

"Me too," I agreed. There must be something I could do besides sit there, hope, and pray. Helplessness was a monster I couldn't shake, no matter how hard I fought it.

I glanced up in time to catch Atlas doing something funny with his face. Was he communicating something to me he didn't want Ms. Pierce to know?

"Excuse me, I need to use the bathroom," I announced, leaning closer to make sure my words reached her.

Martina glanced up at me with motherly concern. She turned to Atlas and pointed a commanding finger. "Would you please be a gentleman and walk with Callie? We don't need anyone else disappearing from this place."

He stood. "Sure."

We took off, our pace fast, until we were several hallways away in a smaller, deserted waiting area.

"Do you think your ex-boyfriend is capable of pulling something like this off? If this wasn't a legit mess up by the hospital, it would take intricate planning and must have had to be enacted right after Trent was admitted."

"Donni's drugged me before, so it makes him my prime suspect for any crime. Do *you* think he took Trent to, took him to...to ki..."

"Don't say it. First, we don't know who did what and why. Let's see what the authorities find out before we go calling the FBI. I just wanted to see what you were thinking."

He went silent, fixing his gaze on the wall above my shoulder. I could feel him thinking.

"You wanted to see if you weren't the only one feeling like this may not be the hospital's fault? Do you think my ex may have something to do with this because of the ongoing feud Donni's determined to have with me and Trent?"

He nodded. "This situation is too strange. We just had that fight. Trent ends up shot the same night. I know a guy who knows a guy who is already checking into this for us. I don't trust the authorities to do a thorough or fast enough job to get this resolved."

I didn't know how to feel. If this wasn't the hospital's mess up, did that mean Trent could be somewhere..."

I swallowed the word, refusing to let my thoughts turn into a weapon against me. I tilted my head to the ceiling in an effort to hold in the cry I wanted to release.

Why was this happening? Why now? I didn't dip my nose in other people's business. I wasn't a messy person. I helped people when I could. Why did I feel like I was being punished?

"He's going to be okay. We are going to find him with or without the authorities," Atlas said with confidence.

I nodded, swallowing enough sorrow to send me clean through to the floor below us. I'd almost lost Trent to a bullet last night, and now he was missing. What could possibly happen next?

Chapter Twenty-six

Callie

The unbearable wait was going to kill me. The hospital, along with the authorities, had sent us all home. We'd had to stop Trent's mother from setting the place on fire as well as keep her from stabbing out the tires of a squad car.

Martina did not play, and if these people didn't find Trent, and soon, the world would no longer be safe from her or me. I fought to control my raging urge to rebel, to yell, to fuck shit up, and I'd kept it together in the eyes of onlookers. Tears were all I'd allowed them to see. However, on the inside, I was one breath away from setting the city on fire.

Even now, as we sat in Dayton's house, I took deep breaths and filled my head with all the good times Trent and I shared during our short courtship.

The wait. Not knowing. I didn't know how much more I could take. I bolted up, making heads jerk in my direction.

"I'm going to go home and shower and change clothes. I'll be back later," I said, flashing a quick glance at the group, whose expressions were clearly asking me if I was crazy.

"We're going with you," Charlene said. "So are we," Atlas agreed, with Ransome nodding in the background.

"I need to be alone for a minute. I'll be careful," I assured them.

"Callie, we don't know where Trent was taken. What if someone *took* him from that hospital? That same someone could be out there waiting to get to you."

I relented at those words, dropping back onto the couch. Were we going to sit here and pretend like we weren't going out of our minds? Trent had been taken from the intensive care unit in a secure hospital. It meant someone risked placing his life in grave danger if they didn't have the means to provide him with proper medical care.

Standing, I lifted calming hands when all eyes landed on me. "Don't worry. I just need to use the restroom."

Several eyes and shoulders dropped, and someone even squeezed out a breath of relief as I marched toward Dayton's bathroom.

***

They were going to kill me. It had only been ten minutes, but I'm sure the group had discovered by now that I'd snuck away from Dayton's house, and she'd figured out I'd stolen her keys. I had to do something.

With every turn I made, doubts crept in and deterred me from what I was about to do. However, the stronger part of my mentality wouldn't allow me to give up my quest. I had to do this. I had to do something to help find Trent.

My phone buzzed, a sign that they had discovered my escape. My friends were resourceful when they needed to be, so they would eventually figure out where I was headed.

Twenty minutes later, I pulled up to Donni's gates. My hands shook when I reached out the window and pushed the button to buzz the house.

"Donni, it's me, Callie. We need to talk."

"Callie," he called, his tone dragging lazily across his tongue like he'd been asleep. A buzz sounded before a click made the gate roll open. The gate moved so slowly, I'd convinced myself to drive off twice. However, I remained, to find answers that would hopefully lead to Trent.

My phone buzzed with a notification that someone was calling. I'd forwarded my calls to go directly to voicemail. I knew who it was and would face my butt chewing like a woman when the time came.

In the midst of contemplating my next move, I pulled forward since the gate had already begun to close. I was probably going to regret doing this, but I had to try for Trent.

Donni opened and stood in the doorway, waiting while I drove up his paved circular driveway. His six-bedroom, five-bathroom mansion was gorgeous, and so were the other expensive material possessions he owned. He'd even bought me a black Mercedes C300 that I hated to give back but had done so when we'd agreed to go our separate ways.

At first, Donni had played the good, decent, nice guy who knew how to have fun, but it was an act to draw me into his life. He started using his material possessions, not his self-worth, as the bargaining tool to keep me. It was further proof that I was with the wrong man.

Now, I was here, on a fishing trip, to find out if he was behind Trent's shooting and disappearance from the hospital.

I exited the car and shoved my phone into the back pocket of my jeans. Donni reached down, aiming to help me up the five steps, but I ignored him.

He dropped his hand, smiling versus commenting on my dismissal. He even eased back a little to allow me to pass by him in peace. Donni was an attractive man, tall, fit, and rich, but he wasn't rich off the foundation of his own hard work.

He was entitled. An only child of rich parents who I found out later used to be in the dope game. He'd used his family's money and street status to convince an aggressive social media world into believing he was a powerful business mogul. The easily influenced didn't need much convincing as they followed him and even aspired to be like him.

I wasn't hating on Donni's hustle as he turned his lie into a practical entertainment business that specialized in celebrity parties and sold tons of merchandise from his online stores.

"Have a seat," he said, ushering his hand toward the large, pale-yellow couch. "Would you like something to drink?"

I'm surprised he didn't keel over from the dangerous side eye I flashed him.

"You actually believe I would take another drink from you?"

He shrugged, unfazed about what he'd done to me.

"I'm here to discuss a situation, and if you are involved, find out what it's going to take for you to stop?"

That statement got his attention.

"What situation are you referring to?"

"Trent was shot last night. He almost died in a drive-by that happened on his block. Was it you?"

His face squinted, tight and fast, while he shook his head.

"Nope. That shit wasn't me. I was never a shooter, not even when I was a dope boy for my family, so don't put that shit on me. I live well. I get money the legal way. Do you think I want to mess all that up over a stripper?"

Was he a good liar, or was I being gullible?

"Callie, look, you're fine and everything. One of the fucking hottest women I've dated, but me trying to kill a motherfucker over you isn't my style."

Why did he sound so convincing?

"You drugged me. It's not a big stretch for you to take out Trent."

He shook his head, swirling the liquor in his glass around before taking a deep swig.

"You got the wrong one in this mess. I can be a little impulsive. Arrogant. Aggressive, but I know better than to put a damn body on my resume."

"That's not all," I told him. "Did you take him from the hospital?"

"What? Callie, are you serious right now? That's some Victor Newman, Young and the Restless soap opera-type shit. If I did take him, you tell me, what the hell would I do with him? If I wanted to beat his ass, I'd walk right up to him and have my guys do it for me."

He took a few steps closer, using his glass as a pointer. "Now, if you want to get rid of all that trouble and discuss us getting back together, we can talk. I love you and everything, always fucking will, but if you're here to blame me for your boyfriend drama, then you can go on and kick rocks."

I stood, getting in his face, hating the way he spoke to me but knowing I wasn't in a position to do anything about it.

"I have one more question."

He cocked an eyebrow.

"Why did you feel the need to drug me? I thought we were better than that. I thought we were on the same page about our break-up."

"I had to try," he shrugged like it wasn't a big deal. "It wasn't the first time I had to give you a little something."

"What!" I yelled.

"Calm down. It was only a little benzodiazepine. I've given you a little in your drinks before. With your work and career and shit, sometimes you were a bit stiff, tense. I'd give you a little something to loosen you up. And despite what you think, I wasn't raping you and shit. I gave you *just* enough to relax, that's all. At the club, I used something different. I didn't know the shit would be that damn strong."

"You do know that you're admitting to a crime, don't you?"

"Callie. Think. Do you remember a time when we were fucking, and it felt like I was *taking* your shit? Did you ever wake up with me fucking you? Did you ever wake up with questions, thinking that I'd done some foul shit to you?"

Damn!

Was he that good a liar, or had I jumped to all the wrong conclusions?

Don't be stupid, Callie, the little voice in my head whispered.

I didn't answer Donni's questions. Instead, I walked off without a word.

"That's what I thought. I hope you find your boyfriend," he called after me in a teasing tone. "I should consider myself lucky because how do you lose a whole man?" he said loud and teasingly behind my back.

All I could think was, *"Let's see if the police are going to ignore me once they hear this recording of you admitting to drugging me multiple times."*

Uncertainty kept me company now. If Donni was telling the truth about not shooting Trent, it meant someone else was stalking him. I didn't believe the hospital had made a transfer error anymore.

I was almost sure this was an abduction. Someone had taken Trent from that hospital, and now I wasn't entirely convinced it was my crazy ex-boyfriend.

Chapter Twenty-seven

Trent

Darkness.

I floated in the dark with nothing to stop me from drifting into space. A twitch. A wiggle. It was all I could muster to shake this overwhelming sense of helplessness. Where was I? Was it daytime? Night? I didn't know what time of day it was, but my swirling memories were reminding me of all that had occurred.

Shot.

Woke up to my angel.

Drugged?

I was dreaming right now, wasn't I? No. I believe I was in the hospital recovering.

Awareness in the form of pain pulled me into a reality I didn't want to face. I struggled to sit up, but my body wouldn't respond. Someone was near. I sensed them, but I couldn't open my heavy eyes for the life of me.

"Callie?" my voice barely sounded above a whisper.

"Your precious Callie isn't here," a female voice said, sounding vaguely familiar.

Pain shot through my eye sockets when I finally opened them and forced myself to see through the dim lighting. The haze began to clear, and a shadow was taking shape. It was a woman. She remained in the shadow of the doorway, staring at me.

"You've always had a thing for chocolate. I could tell it from the beginning, but you were never satisfied with one piece, were you? You had to have a big-ass assorted box filled with different flavors."

Another attempt to sit up made restraints tighten around my wrists with a painful grip. Why was I tied up? Had someone poured a gallon of gas on my chest and tossed a lit match atop it? My eyes fell closed against the throbbing ache ripping me apart before I found the strength to muddle through it.

"I've always been upfront about my intentions with whoever I date. I did nothing wrong. Who are you? Did you drug me?"

A chuckle sounded, and the shadow moved closer.

"You *were* upfront. I'll give you that much, but you also gave me something you couldn't take back or sweet talk your way out of," the woman said, her tone hostile and edgy.

It sounded like she was insinuating that I'd given her a disease. I was a lot of things, diseased wasn't one of them.

"I've never had any type of disease, and I've always protected myself, so if you caught something you couldn't get rid of, it didn't come from me," I managed to say between pained-filled gulps of air.

She chuckled.

"You misinterpreted my statement." She took a few steps closer, which allowed me to see her face.

"Christy?"

She flashed a fake smile that went nowhere near her eyes. Christy was light caramel, and everything about her was too perfect. It should have been my first clue to leave her alone. Perfectly straight teeth, perfectly styled, bone-straight, mid-back length hair. Her clothing was designer everything. Her mind, however, was a landmine of emotional wreckage.

She never shut up about herself and her family and their money, so it became clear from the beginning that she was drowning under the weight of all that financial privilege and not living up to her parents' expectations, which I believed were the main cause of her emotional damage.

"I called you to tell you we had unfinished business," she said. "But you wouldn't give me the time of day. You wouldn't even give me the fucking time to explain to you why we had unfinished business. I also made attempts to see you at the club. And what did you do? You treated me like all those other chicken head hoes you fucked and forgot."

What the hell was she talking about?

"You took me from the hospital because I didn't want to continue a relationship with you?"

Christy's low and sarcastic chuckle sounded despite the merciless pain knifing through me like flaming-hot blades. "Don't flatter yourself, Trent. But you should at least attempt to know who you're climbing into bed with. You never even considered asking me my last name, did you? You fucked me many times in a one-day span of time, and I'll admit, you were the best I've ever had. If you would have entertained the idea of an ongoing relationship, I would have taken the offer. But that's not why you're here. I had to go through all this shit to get your fucking attention so you'd stop ignoring my calls, treating me like a stalker, and listen to what I have to say."

I was smart enough not to say it out loud, but Christy couldn't be described as anything other than a stalker. What the fuck did she think kidnapping someone to have a conversation made her?

I made myself unavailable over the phone and was sometimes hard to reach off-stage, but I wasn't *that* damn hard to find. She made it sound like I had some type of magic shield that kept her from getting to me.

My face squinted so tightly staring at her that I gave myself a headache that added to the aches and pains ravaging my chest cavity.

"Christy, I'm a stripper. You can't blame me for trying to protect myself. Women stalk me. It's a part of the life I've had to learn to live with."

She pursed her lips and rolled her eyes, knowing I had a valid point.

"Whatever," she said, brushing away my statement with a flick of her manicured fingers.

"Are you the one who's been doing all this crazy shit to me and Callie? Stalking us, shooting me, and taking me from the hospital?"

She nodded like doing those things to someone wasn't a big deal. Who the hell was she to think that this was okay? Maybe she was right about me at least needing to know who the hell I was sleeping with. I knew she came from money because she'd talked so incessantly about her family and their wealth that I had stopped listening at some point.

"What's your last name?" I asked her.

"Oh, now you want to know it. After I had to go through all of this to get your attention."

She paused for a long time, standing in place staring at me. I knew lust when I saw it. She wanted me, even now, while I was tied to a bed and seriously injured.

She reached out her hand, intending to officially introduce herself, I supposed. I stared at the hand she offered. Even if I wasn't strapped to the bed, I wouldn't have touched her. I vaguely recalled sleeping with her. I didn't regret it—it just wasn't that memorable.

"Oops, sorry, forgot you're a little tied up right now," she teased. "Anyway, my name is Christy Sylvain of *the* Sylvan family."

My brows shot up high. The Sylvan's had a hand in every type of construction service you could name.

"Yes, those fucking Sylvans. We have more money than the law should allow and, therefore, can get away with all types of shit, including taking you from a hospital."

She snapped her fingers and snickered. "I forgot, there is someone else I'd like to introduce you to. Dear brother," she called out to someone. "Come in here, please."

The man stood in the doorway, much like Christy had. He took slow, deliberate steps, dragging out the agony of my seeing his face.

"Sedric?" I mumbled his name. It was Topaz's fiancé. "You're Christy's brother?"

I swallowed hard. He hated me because I'd slept with Topaz.

"You shot me." It wasn't a question. The looks he'd given me, and the malice he always aimed at me when he saw me at the club was enough to know he wanted to do me harm.

"I told him he was taking things too fucking far. Shooting up and down residential streets like a common thug over a low-rent piece of pussy he could find anywhere."

He spun on his sister, aiming a stiff finger at her face. "You will not talk about Topez that way. You were strung out over this prick after one night, and you have the fucking nerve to tell me about my choices."

She huffed before releasing a loud laugh. "You were ready to kill him for sleeping with that skank. In my opinion, my problem with him is much more important than your little ego trip."

They were two spoiled-ass rich kids using money to get their way, and I was lucky enough to be on both their shit lists. My mother always told me that my dick would get me into a lot of trouble, and here I was, drenched in the middle of a sick plot, so fucked up that it was a grave threat to my life.

"Fuck what you're saying," Christy spit at her brother before she turned to me. "Trent, I didn't want to hurt you. I just wanted your attention so we could finally talk."

"Well, you can get all the attention you want now. We've shot and kidnapped the fucking man," Sedric spit out. She rolled her eyes at him and focused her attention on me.

"I wanted to bring you here because, well..." she stepped off, walked to the door, and cracked it open. Sedric stood, staring after her and shaking his head.

"TJ!" she yelled out. The faint sound of a child's voice responded. Immediately, my head began to shake in the negative.

No!

No fucking way!

The sound of tapping feet growing closer inspired my heart to knock its way through my rib cage to escape my chest.

A little boy, who had to be close to three years old, ran to Christy and jumped into her arms before he slung his small arms around her neck. She stepped closer, her eyes on me, while she nuzzled her nose in the little boy's head of thick black and silky curls. He was clearly bi-racial and...

"Trent, I'd like you to meet TJ." She turned the little boy in her arms so that he was looking down at me. TJ, I'd like you to meet your..."

"Stop right there!" Sedric yelled out. "I love my nephew, and I don't want him all confused and shit. He's being raised by your fiancé and believes that he is his father. Before you go and get his little mind all messed up, you need a DNA test."

What the hell?

She waved her brother off as though him, preventing her from confusing her child, and me for that matter, was no big deal. She stared at her brother for a long time, contemplating his suggestion before focusing her attention on me.

"TJ, I'd like you to meet your Uncle Trent."

"Uncle Tent. Uncle Tent," the little boy called down, reaching for me and flashing rows of tiny teeth.

"Baby, your uncle's not feeling well. He can't hold you right now," she said, her eyes zeroing in on me, nodding at the little boy.

"Trent, this is why I kept trying to talk to you." Her face squinted into a tight knot, and she leaned closer. She ran probing eyes over me as I fought to stay focused.

"You don't look so good," she stated the obvious.

No shit.

"Anyway," she said, casting aside the hint of empathy I saw flash in her gaze. "This is the reason I was looking for you. It wasn't because I was trying to get back with you or anything."

"Bullshit," her brother coughed into his hand, calling her attention, but my eyes remained pinned on the little boy who continued to reach for me.

His eyes. They were like mine, hazel-green. He also possessed the same *something* else I couldn't put my finger on, but I sensed it just the same.

Was I a father or not? If her brother hadn't made the statement about a DNA test, I would have bought her story without question. Now, the pressure of not knowing or having to wait to find out would be a silent killer.

Why else would she go through all this trouble if she wasn't sure I was the baby's father?

Sedric approaching us was all that broke up the staring contest taking place between Christy and me, while TJ attempted to climb from her arms to get to me.

"Are you done?" Sedric asked Christy. "You got what you wanted, and now that you've had your little family reunion, it's my turn."

She jerked her neck at him, her face frowning.

"Don't you think you've done enough? You shot him. What more do you want?"

He didn't answer, but the deadly gleam in his eyes said he wanted me un-alive.

"No," Christy said, turning to block me from Sedric's view. "I can't let you hurt my baby's....*uncle*."

"Why? Because you still have feelings for this stripper motherfucker?"

"Curse word," TJ pointed out to his uncle.

"Sorry neph', Uncle's just a little...upset," he said, ruffling the boy's curls while peeking around to send an evil glare in my direction.

"I'm not going to kill him. I just want him to wish that he was dead. When I'm done with him, you can do whatever it is you believe you need to do with him."

They were talking about me like I wasn't even a person. I should have been used to being treated this way, but I wasn't. Were they planning to keep me as their prisoner?

If I was sleeping, right now would be the perfect time for me to wake the hell up. If I wasn't, I had no idea how to get myself out of this situation. Even if I wasn't tied up, I was too weak to run or fight.

Them letting me go meant they ran the risk of me going to the police. If they kept me as a prisoner, eventually, they would have to let me go, or I'd find a way to escape. The only other choice was *death*.

My eyes slammed shut, and I squeezed them against the ache rattling around in my head and wreaking havoc on the rest of me. Although my mind was a battlefield of detonating bombs, I continued my attempt to come up with a way to convince them to let me go. It was too bad that nothing convincing came to mind.

Lord, if you still hear this sinner's prayers, please have mercy on me.

Chapter Twenty-eight

Trent

Pain.

It kept taking me to the brink of my tolerance, and when my body would reach the point of giving up, the pain ebbed enough to bring me back from the point of passing out.

The drama. The unbelievable aspect of the situation in which I was trapped. If pain wasn't my reality, my alarm clock, and my torturer, I would chalk this all up to being a realistic dream.

"You aren't fucking touching him. What if you kill him this time?"

Christy shouted loud enough for her son, my potential son, to cover his little ears.

"What the fuck do you think we're supposed to do with him now? He's seen our faces. The moment we let him go, he goes to the police, and you go to jail."

"Me. How am I the one who's going to jail? Your dumb ass shot him?"

"And I've told you for the hundredth time that it was an accident. I was just trying to scare him. Besides, you're the one who wanted to kidnap him, but never considered what would happen once he was set free?"

She turned back, her face squeezed in frustration. "Here, hold your son," she said, sitting TJ in the bed next to me, and turning back to do battle with her brother. Thankfully, TJ was at my side and not on my aching chest.

"Hi, buddy, you want to lie here with me?" I asked him. He nodded and flashed me a smile that barely broke the surface of his lips. He was exhausted, his eyes heavy, his small body swaying.

I couldn't use my arms to adjust him, but the little boy knew what to do. He crawled across my restrained arm and settled in the nook connecting the side of my burning chest and my shoulder.

This was the first time since I woke up that the pain emanating from my injuries was cast aside, because the impact of this moment stole it.

Am I holding my son?

He settled his head within the bend of my shoulder and rested his little hand at my side. It didn't take but a handful of seconds for his heavy eyes to start fluttering, the lure of sleep tempting enough to pull him under.

If this was my son, how would it affect my relationship with Callie? Would she understand that this was as much a surprise to me as it would be to her? Given my current situation, was I going to even see Callie again?"

When the haunting idea threatened to repeat its taunting echo in my head, a dead, almost calming silence pulled at my demented reality and sucked me under.

***

Callie

They are going to kill me. Charlene and Dayton were going to kill me for taking off. When I pulled up, I noticed that Atlas' car was no longer in the driveway. A deep breath and a long exhale prepared me to ring Dayton's doorbell.

The door snatched open so hard, I jumped back. A perfectly manicured hand reached out and snatched my ass by the collar.

"Get your ass in this house and give me my damn keys," Dayton said, snatching her car keys from my hand. I felt like a kid who knew they had done wrong and was terrified of catching the whipping I deserved.

Charlene aimed a finger toward the bathroom. "I need to use the bathroom," she said before she stepped off in that direction.

"The police and the hospital's been calling. They found a lead and are deploying a team to see if Trent is at the place they suspect," Dayton said, her words rushed. "Atlas and Ransome found out the address somehow and are taking their asses over there. I hope they don't do something stupid and keep the police from doing their jobs."

My mouth fell open and stayed that way, as all of that information bounced around in my head. Dayton jiggled her keys restlessly.

"Charlene! Hurry up and drop that water. We gotta go!"

"Go?" I asked.

"Yes. Go," Dayton said. "You don't think we're going to sit here in this house and wait patiently, do you? I made Atlas give up that address. They've only been gone for about ten minutes. So if Charlene ever finishes peeing, we can go and get your shot up and kidnapped man."

"I'm finished," Charlene said, rubbing lotion into her hands. "Let's go."

Meanwhile, the shocking words Dayton had just spoken continued slapping me in the face, while I followed them through Dayton's front door, my steps choppy.

Once I stumbled into the back seat of Dayton's car, still warm from my little road trip, I sat back and prayed. Trent was alive. He would be saved from whoever took him. I would see him again. Touch and hug and kiss him again. Tell him that I loved him. I believed with all my heart and soul that Trent was okay and healthy. I couldn't take any more bad news, or I just might crack.

"Don't think you're not going to get these words I have for you about your little field trip, Callie." Dayton kicked off the ass-chewing session I knew she and Charlene had for me. "I tracked my car. I know where your lil' wanna-be-detective ass went."

"That ex-boyfriend lunatic of yours could have killed you," Charlene added. The disappointment in her tone wasn't missed.

"What if he was the one who took Trent from that hospital? What if he wasn't the one who took Trent but was maybe smart enough to have someone else do it for him?" Dayton questioned, and I instinctively knew these were not the kinds of questions she expected me to answer.

Charlene turned around from the passenger seat. "What were you thinking? We would have come with you. You know we wouldn't have let you go to that psycho by yourself, right?" She eyeballed me, waiting for an answer.

Biting into my lip, I nodded as tears stung the backs of my eyes. These ladies were the kinds of friends many dreamed of, and I was lucky enough to have them in my life.

I knew they would have gone with me to confront Donni. I also knew they would have raised hell and started all types of mess. There was no way I was allowing them to get into trouble because I'd hitched myself to the wrong man.

"Thank you. I know you would have come with me,"
I finally blurted my cracked words. "But, Trent and I have
had so much drama swirling around us that I didn't want
you getting involved any deeper."

Charlene turned to reach through the space between
the seats to take my hand. Dayton took one of her hands
off the steering wheel and reached back so that I could
hold both their hands.

"In the infamous words of Gee Money from New
Jack City, 'We all we got,'" Dayton announced.

"Don't ever think you have to do anything on your
own. We're here for you. No matter what," Charlene
added.

"Thank you. I appreciate you two more than I can say
right now," I choked out, my chest tight and heavy.

Flashing lights caught our eyes, and our hand-holding
sermon came to an abrupt end.

I jerked around in the seat, trying to figure out where
the hell we were. I'd been too far inside my own head to
pay attention.

"Are we in…"

"Sherwood Forest," Charlene finished. It was a little
town right outside of Richmond, so close, it should have
been a part of the city.

"They're inside a cupcake shop?" I asked, frowning
at the location Charlene pointed out.

"Not any old cupcake shop. Have you ever had one
of those delicious, expensive, melt in your mouth…"

Charlene shoved Dayton. "Really? Sometimes I wonder about your mental stability. You do remember why
we're driving up here with all these lights flashing and
cops…"

Charlene's rant stopped abruptly because six, seven, eight SWAT team members ran across the road from an adjacent alley to the Cupcake shop. Three carried a large metal battering ram. It was like seeing something straight from an action movie.

Dayton brought the car to a screeching halt, not only because we were hundreds of feet away from an active police raid but because of the barricade that was set up across the highway.

He's going to be okay.

He has to be okay.

He will be okay.

Three thunderous rams and the pink and blue front door of the shop splintered open, sending small chips of wood and dust particles flying into the air. The team filed in with guns raised, discarding the battering ram with parts of the splintered door. Another team of about eight waited behind strategically placed squad cars and barricades they had set up.

The stiff tension stirring in the air gripped me so tightly that I couldn't move. I couldn't speak. I was damn near suffocating on my anxiety.

Why were they taking so long? It felt like they had been in there for hours, although I was sure it had only been minutes.

Please. God. Please.

I wasn't the most religious person, but I did believe in God and read the bible occasionally. I was one of those people who was guilty of calling on Him in times of trouble without checking in with him all the time.

Bodies began to file out of the broken door of the cupcake shop, but I didn't see Trent. Where was he? He didn't deserve this, to be robbed, shot down in his own driveway, stolen from the hospital in critical condition, and now...

"Is that Trent?" Dayton yelled, leaning into the steering wheel. I damn near jumped into the front seat, falling into the middle passageway to get a look. Charlene attempted to help me get myself up, but I kept slipping back into the opening because I couldn't pull my straining eyes off the sight of the three men who'd stepped through the broken door. They carried a man between them.

Trent!

I struggled like a stuck pig to pull myself from between the seats and managed after several harsh jerks. I wobbled in the seat, rolling toward the back passenger door. Once I had a good grip on the handle, I pulled hard and kicked it open before hopping out like I was auditioning to become a member of the SWAT team who'd busted down the cupcake shop's door. I took off, hopping the barricade like an Olympic hurdle jumper.

"Callie, slow down!"

"Callie!"

Charlene and Dayton yelled after me, hot on my trail.

"You can't just go...."

Click! Click! Clank! Clack!

"Stop right there!" The police yelled.

I froze, lifting my hand. Dayton bumped into my back, her hands lifting along with Charlene's, who stood at my other side.

With high-powered weapons aimed at us, I should have been more fearful, but my focus was on Trent being carried between those officers.

"That's my boyfriend," I called out, moving my hand to point in Trent's direction.

Trent lifted his head, and even in the dimness that encircled him I saw the pain emanating from the tight creases in his face and gritted teeth.

"Please...let them in," Trent called out, pain in every word.

I didn't wait until the officers dropped their guns. I took off and ran to Trent, taking him from the much stronger man's arms. He leaned into my waiting arms, even managing to brush a soft kiss onto my cheek.

Epilogue

Callie

A month later.

"Dayton, I love you, but I can't go on a girl's trip now. I just spent two weeks on the road with Twisted Minds after spending weeks before that taking care of my man. Now that he's recovering well, we intend to go somewhere nice and peaceful, like a deserted island," I said to Dayton with Charlene listening in on the other line. We were on our usual three-way call if we weren't planning to see each other for the weekend.

Trent's mother had stuck around to help me take care of him. It had taken an act of congress for him to convince her that he was healthy enough for her to return to California.

"Romance. Couples time. And love and all that shit. What's the purpose? It's mind-fuckery at its finest. A life goal for others. For you and Charlene, I believe it is lust clouding your judgment. I mean, I can't blame you based on the choices you made, but when the smoke clears, you'll eventually come to your senses." Dayton said.

She believed she was speaking some sort of dating prophecy. I laughed, long and hard enough to get Dayton's non-committal ass to join me. She was convinced that mine and Charlene's minds were clouded with lust and was praying that we'd eventually come to our senses.

"Trust me on this, Dayton, if you ever meet the right one, you will eat every word you just spat at me." I laughed.

"Yeah. Whatever. Since you and Charlene have traded in this stallion for the two Shetland ponies you're intent on keeping, I'm going to binge on some *GOT* and order Chinese. Can't get more romantic than that," Dayton stated.

I laughed even harder. I was a fan of the show, and if she found the level of gruesome violence it displayed romantic, I feared my friend was crazier than I assumed.

"Bye, Callie. Bye, Charlene," she said, hanging up before I could get another word in. I bid Charlene a good night before turning to the handsome man grinning at my side. I leaned in for a kiss that he graciously bestowed.

"What was that for?" Trent asked, his smile wider than my couch.

"Just because you're here with me."

I would have to run at least twenty miles to get these ice cream, chips, chocolate, and wine calories off, but it was worth it. My and Trent's movie nights were one of the best times we shared together, and they always led to our best sex sessions.

The envelope on the table before us would make this night different, but it could no longer be avoided. We'd put this off for two days now. I wasn't sure if what was inside would add another heavy injection of drama into our lives.

"Can I ask you something?"

Trent nodded. "Anything."

"When you were in the cellar of that cupcake shop, and Christy informed you that you were a father, how did the news make you feel?"

He squeezed his forehead before picking up the remote and muting the television. Turning in my direction, he stared into my eyes.

"At first, I assumed it was a lie—that she was using that innocent kid to persuade me to be with her. It wasn't her who made me think deep and hard about what the possibility of having a child meant. It was the little boy himself. His innocent eyes. When he stared into my eyes, I considered that he hadn't asked to be in that situation. He certainly didn't need a mother crazy enough to drag him into her crime scene."

Trent paused, his shoulders lifting and falling with his sigh and his eyes closed. I was sure, wading through the horrific events that occurred that night.

"Christy and Sedric argued, slinging words like punches, so she sat TJ next to me on the bed. He felt safe enough to cuddle up to me and lay his little head against my side. Everything about him was still so innocent, like she hadn't taken that away from him yet. We lay there silently while angrily tossed words filled the space. I made a vow to myself that if I were his father, if I ever had kids of my own, I would never do anything that could hurt them mentally or physically. I would protect their happiness even at the cost of my own life. Even now, I'm grateful that he's in the custody of his grandparents."

Trent had relayed to me what happened that night, but he hadn't gone into vivid details like this. I took his hand, kissed the back, and kept it pinned between mine.

"You asked how the news of possibly being a father made me feel. At first, I was terrified. I even prayed that it wasn't true. It was strange, and it weirded me out. I also felt unlucky. But when TJ laid his little head against the side of my chest, all of those other feelings disappeared. I wanted to protect him even if I wasn't his biological father."

The sentiment caused tears to sting the backs of my eyes. Silence loomed over us until Trent took a slow, deep breath. It was time. We lifted our gazes again to the envelope that neither of us had been brave enough to pick up.

"You open it," Trent said, nodding toward the envelope.

Lifting my arm was a task, but I shoved it forward and reached out my hand to pick up and open the envelope.

The words filled my view and appeared to lift off the page as my brain decoded them. I could feel Trent's eyes boring a hole in me.

"Trenton Pierce, you are not excluded. The probability that you are the biological father is 99.9%."

He didn't move, didn't breathe, but stared straight ahead.

"I don't know how to feel. I don't know what to say," he mumbled.

I reached out, took his hand, and squeezed.

"It's okay to be happy, Trent, and after what you just shared about TJ, I'm sincerely happy for you."

He finally moved and turned toward me with hope peeking from within the depth of his gaze.

"You're happy...for me?"

There was confusion in the tone he'd used to ask the question. It was also etched into the creases of his forehead and seeping from his gaze.

"I have a child with another woman. It wasn't intentional, but..."

"But nothing," I cut him off. "I was grown enough to look past your job and see *you* so that I could love *you*. I'm also grown enough to know that TJ needs you in his life. Besides, his mother's in jail, and after what she pulled, I don't think even their family's high-powered attorney is going to be able to keep her from a long prison sentence. She broke several laws and kidnapped you from a hospital and was in the car with her brother when he shot you."

Trent nodded, placing his hands over his mouth, and I couldn't tell if he was fighting not to laugh or cupping a genuine smile.

"We aren't the perfect couple by any stretch of the imagination, but I'm going to be there for you and TJ," I promised.

"Callie," he whispered, grasping my hand and staring with tender flecks of awe and gratitude sparking in his gaze. He scooted to the edge of the couch and carefully dropped to the floor. He winced while positioning himself before me, still not fully recovered. Despite his pain, he reached up and took my face in his palms.

"You truly mean that, don't you?"

I nodded. "I mean every word, but make no mistake, Trenten Pierce, if you ever cross me, ever put our relationship in jeopardy, ever cause me to shed anything but happy tears, I'll make what Christy and Sedric did to you look like a field trip."

His mouth dropped open before he let a smile slide across his lips. "I understand. Besides, I've met your friends. They've already laid down their threats if I do anything to hurt you. One promised to snatch every last bone out of my body, and I believed her. Trust me, I don't want you or them coming after me."

I chuckled, picturing Dayton and Charlene threatening him on my behalf.

He ran a tender finger over my cheek.

"I love you, Callie, more than you could ever know."

I leaned in, thinking he was about to kiss me, but I was wrong. He reached down and came up with a little blue box that had me fighting to catch my next breath. My mouth dropped open wide and stayed that way.

Magical moments were something I read about in romance novels, something I saw on television shows, not something I ever envisioned for myself. I never believed I would receive any of the magical things this world had to offer. Trent's love was the first—now this. My shaky hand covered my open mouth when he flicked the box open.

"Callie Dayana Hendrix, will you marry me?"

I gripped my throat, massaging my neck in an attempt to make my voice work. I didn't know I was crying until I saw the droplets catching the light and falling onto my lap.

I nodded. "Yes," I croaked out. "Yes!" I yelled.

My hand shook so badly that Trent clamped his hand around mine to ease the ring on. I didn't get a good look at the ring through my tears. Honestly, I didn't care how it looked. I could look at it later. All I wanted was Trent. I threw myself into his arms, crying into his shoulder while he grinned into mine.

"I love you too," I finally whispered between my joyous giggles and happy tears.

End of Love Whispered

Blind Date with a Book

Don't feel like shopping around for your next read? Grab yourself a Blind Date with a Book.

All you have to do is head on over to (https://www.michelewesley.com/category/all-products) pick a genre and leave the rest to me, Author Keta Kendric.

If this is your first time reading my books, Blind Date with a Book, is a fun way of introducing yourself to more of my books. If you've already read my books, I appreciate you, and offer blind book dates by other best-selling authors.

Birthday, holiday, or just-because, Blind Dates with a Book are great gift ideas for yourself, your book friends, or loved ones. These hot Blind Dates arrive in the mail autographed and beautifully wrapped with swag.

Head on over to my Website Shop where you can use the coupon code HOTDATE15 to get 15% off on your order.

Note: Also offering regular autographed paperback books if a blind date is not your cup of tea.

Author's Note

Readers, my sincere thank you for reading Love Whispered. Please leave a review or star rating letting me and others know what you thought of the book. If you enjoyed it please check out the next books in the series. If you enjoyed any of my other books, please pass them along to friends or anyone you think would enjoy them.

Other Titles by Keta Kendric

The Twisted Minds Series:

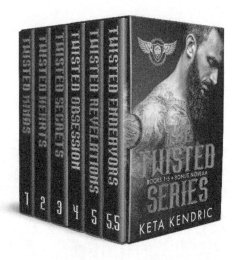

The Twisted Box Set

The Chaos Series:

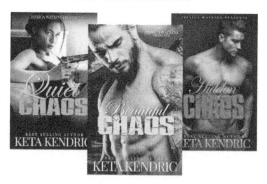

Beautiful Chaos #1
Quiet Chaos #2
Hidden Chaos#3

The Love Series

<u>Love Lied #1</u>
<u>Love Whispered #2</u>
<u>Love Lingered #3</u>

Stand Alones:

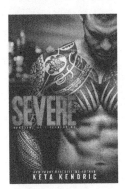

<u>Severe</u>

Roots of the Wicked

Primo DeLuca

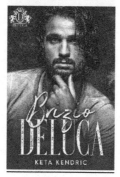

Brizio DeLuca

Novellas:

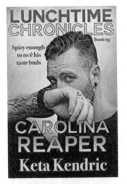

Carolina Reaper

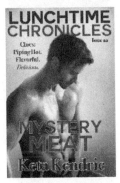

Mystery Meat

Spice Cake

Paranormals:

Sevyn

Smoke

The Box

Kindle Vella:

Love Lied Series

Audiobooks:

Connect on Social Media

Subscribe to my Newsletter or Paranormal Newsletter for exclusive updates on new releases, sneak peeks, and much more.

You can also follow me on:

Newsletter Sign up: https://mailchi.mp/c5ed185fd868/httpsmailchimp

Paranormal Newsletter Sign up: https://mailchi.mp/38b87cb6232d/keta-kendric-paranormal-newsletter

Instagram: https://instagram.com/ketakendric

Facebook Readers' Group: https://www.facebook.com/groups/380642765697205/

BookBub: https://www.bookbub.com/authors/keta-kendric

Twitter: https://twitter.com/AuthorKetaK

Goodreads: https://www.goodreads.com/user/show/73387641-keta-kendric

TikTok: https://www.tiktok.com/@ketakendric?

Pinterest: https://www.pinterest.com/authorslist/

Made in the USA
Middletown, DE
26 August 2024

59310928R00159